The Earl and Miss Muffet

Regency Ever After Book Three

ANNEKA R. WALKER

Copyright © 2025 by Anneka R. Walker

All rights reserved.

No unauthorized use of any portion of this book may be used to train generative artificial intelligence technologies (AI).

The story, all names, characters, places, and incidents portrayed in this publication are a product of the author's imagination or are used fictitiously. Any resemblance to any person (living or dead) is entirely coincidental.

No part of this publication may be reproduced without prior written permission from the publisher or author, except to be used as a quotation for a book review.

Dedication

To the anxious ones,

May faith and love triumph over all your fears.

Little Miss Muffet sat on a tuffet,
Eating her curds and whey;
Along came a spider, who sat down beside her,
And frightened Miss Muffet away!

Chapter 1

ELENA COWERED UNDER HER twin sister's icy glare. Bianca pointed her sharp fingernail at Elena's chest, her lips pulled into a sneer. "How dare you solicit attention from any man before I am married. You know the rules."

A step backward put Elena against the far wall of her bedchamber. Elena knew the rules and had made many concessions to follow them. She searched for words to explain herself. Could she be blamed when a man spoke to her? Elena never met his eyes or answered his questions, but Bianca would not care. The tip of Bianca's fingernail jabbed Elena just under her collarbone, and she winced. "Please, Bianca. You know I did not betray you."

"Do I?"

If looks could kill, Elena would have died already. "I promise. I never said a word to him!"

Bianca released her pressure and stepped back. "Fine, I believe you." Then she reached forward and grabbed a lock of Elena's hair and snipped it off with a pair of scissors Elena had not even seen hiding in Bianca's other hand.

Elena whimpered. "Stop, please, no more!"

Bianca laughed and tossed the toffee-brown curl at Elena's feet. She stalked from the room like she was the Queen of England—perhaps Bloody Mary herself.

Elena shuttered. Being twins with a competitive sister had been hard as a child, but it was far worse now. She picked up the lifeless curl and dropped it on her dressing table. With a sigh, she pinned the shorter hair back so the damage was no longer noticeable. Bianca had always bullied her, but this fixation with marrying first had led to more extreme behavior.

Elena grabbed her penknife off her writing desk and went to a panel on the wall by her bed, prying it open with the small blade. It popped out easily since it had been done so many times over the years. Elena slipped her journal out and carried it to her desk. After Bianca made her point, she generally left Elena to herself. This was when Elena scribbled down her thoughts, desperate to purge her emotions. No one else could hear her complaints.

Father did not even love his own wife—so why care for his daughter? Mother . . . Elena sighed. Mother could not control Bianca any more than Elena could. Elena had long felt that Mother favored Bianca too, which did not help the situation. Bianca twisted everything to construe Elena as the villain. Kind governesses had often intervened, but now that they had outgrown them, life for Elena had become miserable. Every time Mother sided with Bianca, Elena lost the desire to defend herself—eventually, giving up on it completely. It was better to keep the peace and suffer with a degree of patience, knowing Bianca would capture an innocent young man's attention soon enough, and then Elena would be free.

She finished recording Bianca's latest cruelty and slipped the lock of hair in between the pages as evidence. She slipped the book inside the wall and replaced the panel. Not that it mattered if she kept a record, but Elena knew she could not keep her emotions bottled up without some reprieve. Her heart had begun to flutter from the constant anxiety, and writing helped in a small way.

A knock sounded on her door. Not wanting to draw attention to her secret, Elena moved away from the wall just as Mother stepped inside the room.

"Elena, Bianca said you threatened her with the scissors. Please tell me it isn't true."

Bianca might be insufferable, but she was smart. Why punish Elena once when she could do it twice? "No, Mother. I meant to snip a loose thread from her dress is all. I hope she did not think . . ."

"Yes, she did." Mother pinched her lips tight. "I am at my wits' end. I gave you one last chance at the house party at Rosewood Park a few months ago, but you did not even try to converse with anyone. I cannot justify paying for another Season for you. It would be better if you stayed at home while your sister and I go to London next year."

Elena wanted to rejoice at the news, but she bowed her head instead. "I will stay behind and do penance." To be parted from Bianca for however many months parliament was in session would be sheer heaven!

Mother rubbed a spot above her brow. "How am I blessed with two beautiful daughters who don't appreciate each other?"

"See to Bianca's needs," Elena said simply.

Mother dropped her hand and eyed Elena with uncertainty. "I can never understand how such a sweet, meek child could bully her sister. And always when I am not around." Her mother often remarked on the unusual nature Elena possessed, but Elena did her best to earn her mother's respect in whatever way she could—even if it meant humbly accepting her punishments.

She sighed. "Missing London is not enough. You have forced my hand. I am sending you to stay with a friend of mine. Bianca will be punished unnecessarily, as she dotes on social opportunities, and you shall be punished by being forced into one. I will not be there for you to hide behind."

Elena's heart raced. She put her hand over it to still the pressure in her chest. She wanted to plead for a chance to leave Bianca, but she needed to show remorse, not enthusiasm. She lowered her eyes and softly said, "If you wish it, Mother."

Mother clasped her hands together. "You are to leave right away to visit Lady Crawford."

Elena's eyes widened at the name. She blinked rapidly. No, no, no. This could not be right. "Lady Crawford? The mother of...?"

"You have guessed the connection. You met her sons at the house party you attended at Rosewood Park, but she has a daughter about your age too—Lady Mary."

Elena had spent the entire party avoiding the family, so she could barely claim an acquaintance. Mr. Hadley, the younger son, had attempted to speak to her, but the older son, Lord Crawford, had been far too distinguished to waste his breath on her. "Surely, it would inconvenience such an important family."

Mother sighed. "I would never presume to intrude on the late earl's wife, but my friend has an unusually soft disposition and agreed to have you as her guest for one month. She is nothing but discreet."

Elena dipped her head in defeat, and this time, it was not an act. "I will go if it is what you wish." It seemed vastly unfair for her chance at freedom to be at the house of Lord Crawford. He'd been in hot pursuit of Miss Bliss at their house party, spouting poetry at every opportunity, only to be disappointed when Miss Bliss fell for his brother. He was handsome, but that and his title would serve as a constant reminder of her inferiority. What if he thought she had come to pursue him? She wrung her hands together. It would be humiliating for them both.

"I am desperate for you two girls to get along," Mother said, interrupting Elena's panicky thoughts. "Time apart will help you appreciate your sister more. I daresay, I will regret sending you at all once Bianca hears of this. She would love a chance to spend more time with such an influential family and will be very put out, but it is you who needs the exposure and guidance. For this reason, I must ask you to keep this trip to yourself."

Elena blinked back the tears threatening to spill over. "Yes, Mother."

"Good. I will accept Lady Crawford's invitation, which gives you a week to prepare yourself. On the day of your departure, I will distract Bianca with a shopping trip and arrange a carriage to arrive while we are in town. When you return, I pray you will put these wicked ways behind you."

Mother turned to leave, and silent tears finally escaped down Elena's cheeks. All the pressures of her little world had driven her to a precipice, and this trip felt like a firm push off the edge. She never walked to town unattended, voiced her opinion in public, or spoke of scholarly subjects reserved for men. She strictly obeyed the moral code and protected her reputation as a lady at all costs. Such was the fate of their gender. It was a stifling lifestyle for some, but Elena could manage well if these were her only rules to guide herself by.

Bianca had forced her to follow an even stricter guideline. She was forbidden to paint, sing, or perform a musical instrument. She could never play cards, recite poetry, or even speak while in society. Thankfully, she could embroider and read without any fuss since those sorts of activities could be performed quietly. Any public discretion earned her Bianca's wrath.

Had she not suffered enough all these years? She knew Mother felt some affection for her, but all she ever saw was her disappointment. With a visit to Lady Crawford, whose sons already knew of her pathetic existence, dare she even hope for a reprieve?

Chapter 2

A FAR WINDOW WAS propped open in the drawing room of Banbury Castle, letting in an August breeze Anton could appreciate. He'd rather not be hot during an already uncomfortable situation. He sat across from his younger brother, sister, and best friend on one of three sofas situated around an empty fireplace. Mother had gathered them to greet Miss Muffet who had just arrived.

"I must warn you," Blake Gunther said to Anton's sister, Mary, "Miss Muffet is a total bore." Gunther might be his soon-to-be brother and closest friend, but he deserved the slap on his shoulder he received from Mary.

"Don't be rude." Mary shook her head and turned to face Anton.

"Trust me," Gunther said, fluffing his blond hair up off his forehead. "If you had been with her at the house party with your brothers and me, then you would understand. The woman does not engage in cards, play croquet, dance, or even speak."

"Of course she speaks." Mary laughed, her dark curls bouncing.

Unfortunately, this was how Anton remembered Miss Muffet too. "The only thing I have seen her do is sit down for meals, but I would not be surprised if she was too timid to eat."

His brother, Terrance, reached forward and grabbed a handful of nuts from a decorative bowl on the tea tray. "I tried to engage her in conversation once or twice, but she said very little and did not appreciate my efforts." He sat back and stretched out his long legs, dropping nuts into his mouth one at a time.

Anton tapped Terrance's foot with his own. Time to get his family on board. "Miss Muffet might be as dull as dishwater, but I expect all of you to make her feel welcome here. Mama is completely exhausted from her trip and overwhelmed with two weddings on the horizon. We cannot expect her to play hostess around the clock."

"You mean for us to take turns?" Mary asked.

"An excellent idea," Anton said. "Who shall be first?"

Gunther scooted closer in his seat to Mary. "Since Mary and I are engaged, I shall assist her in her turn."

"And it isn't very proper for me to entertain her," Terrance argued. "Miss Bliss would never permit it." Anton tightened his hand on the arm of his chair. He had once thought Miss Bliss would be his fiancé, not his brother's. Any mention of her name still bothered him.

"You can still visit with Miss Muffet after dinner," Anton said, attempting to keep his voice even. "When Miss Bliss arrives, you can join forces like Gunther and Mary."

Terrance wiped his forehead in relief like he'd escaped the guillotine. It looked like entertaining Miss Muffet would largely fall to Anton. He had more than enough to do running the estate and trying to get everything in order before another session of parliament. He had tenant problems and harvest looming. He needed to chaperone two engaged couples and now this. He pulled at his cravat. Someone had better open up a second window. He longed for fresh air. "All right," he said, shifting in his seat, "do not forget your charges."

"Yes, Father," Terrance teased.

Anton picked up a nut from the tea tray and threw it at his brother just as Terrance turned away. It nailed him in the back of the head.

"Ouch!" Terrance cried.

"My apologies." Anton smiled. "Your large head makes a perfect target."

Terrance smirked. "I'll return the favor when you least expect it." They had never grown out of their brotherly pranks, so the threat was not a surprise.

"You might be taller," Anton said, "but I am superior in my brother-torture skill set. It comes with age. A baby like you could never understand." The insults were harmless, but they reminded him that he really did care about his brother—even if he was getting married before him. He was quickly losing everything of normalcy around him. It had been hard when Father died, but having his brother and sister marry and leave him behind might be worse.

The door opened, and they stood on ceremony. Mother guided Miss Muffet into the room. The bespectacled creature kept her head ducked and slightly turned away from them. Never had Anton met someone so painfully shy before.

"You remember my sons, Lord Crawford and Mr. Hadley?" Mother motioned to him and Terrance. They bowed like well-practiced soldiers—and just as serious. How could they not be under such awkward circumstances?

"How do you do?" Anton asked.

Miss Muffet, in her dowdy, shapeless gray dress curtsied, low and deep. She avoided his eyes and made no verbal greeting.

"And this is my daughter Lady Mary and her intended, Mr. Gunther. But you have met Mr. Gunther before. He lives a few miles away, and we see him quite regularly."

Miss Muffet curtsied without further acknowledgment.

Mary stepped forward. "I do hope we will be good friends, Miss Muffet."

Miss Muffet murmured something they could not hear.

Mother looked at Anton for help. She seemed weary in body and spirit, having not quite recovered from her recent journey to care for his older sister and her children.

Anton cleared his throat and approached Miss Muffet. "Would you care for a tour of Banbury Castle?" He put his arm out as a not-so-subtle hint.

She tentatively accepted his arm, and Anton realized what he had done. He had volunteered to be alone with the silent woman. Heaven help him.

Terrance gave Anton an amused glance as he led Miss Muffet past him and out of the drawing room. Anton showed Miss Muffet the dining room, the ballroom, the portrait gallery, and finally, they stepped into Banbury's library. A small fire crackled in the hearth and filled the room with more warmth than he liked this time of year. Besides his office, this was his domain.

The rows of books felt more alive than some people. If only their unspoken words could burst their spines and teach him all their wisdom and knowledge. He admired the room for a moment, proud of his collection, then turned to gauge the level of disinterest from Miss Muffet. Instead of tucking her chin down and ignoring him altogether, her attention was consumed with her surroundings. Anton caught a full picture of her profile and blinked in surprise. Lands, she had very fine skin. She extended her neck to see the books on the highest shelf, flush with the ceiling. He caught himself staring at the slender curve of her throat.

He looked away, uncomfortable with the idea of finding such a woman attractive. Dare he mention that this was his private library? It would be a lie, but if he had to share it, he didn't want it to be with Miss Muffet. His sister, Mary, rarely read unless it was a letter from a friend. Terrance enjoyed history and geography and the farmer's almanac, but he did not have much of an imagination. So, the library was Anton's solace from the world. He cleared his throat. "Do you care for books, Miss Muffet?" What a silly question. He recalled her complete absorption in books at Rosewood Park during their house party.

"Yes." Her answer was so quiet, he nearly missed it.

It was a small triumph, which encouraged him to press her. "Oh? Would you care to borrow a book?"

"Perhaps another time." Her words were so light they could be carried out the window with the breeze. She turned to leave the library, and his impatience with her grew. He predicted this to be the longest month of his life.

Elena skipped around her bedchamber the next morning, then twirled and fell on her bed. So, this was what heaven was like. She was free here in her room, and it was glorious. The tour of Banbury had been fascinating. It was an actual medieval castle, albeit a renovated one, with a portion of its original moat channeling off into the Oxford Canal. Nonetheless, it had a keep, an outer wall, and an elaborate ornamental garden—all of which were perfectly wonderful for someone as passionate for history as she was. The town was built off of its property as an appendage, rather like a hen watching over its chicks.

Her smile dropped, thinking of what had come after the tour. Dinner had been less thrilling with her conflicting inner voices telling her how she must behave. It was as if Bianca was inside of her, commanding her to follow her rules. Elena blinked away her ugly thoughts. After a full day with her host family yesterday, she refused to think of Bianca. This was a moment to savor.

Unfortunately, her first task of the day would be to make a list of excuses to avoid the family. The less interaction, the less fuel Bianca could use against her. After she pondered a few ideas, she made her way to the dining room for breakfast. She almost turned around when she saw Lord Crawford, his lean figure bent over his food, eating alone. Her eyes went to his neatly combed dark hair and his stylish double-knotted cravat. She stepped backward, but he caught sight of her. Instinctively, she dropped her gaze.

"Did you sleep well?" he asked.

What was she supposed to say? *Yes, infinitely better than at home where my sister plots how to stage my premature death*? Instead, she chanced a quick nod. She quietly moved to the sideboard and began to fill her plate with a hardboiled egg, dried dates, and a slice of sweet bread.

She sat as far from Lord Crawford as she could. She moved to take a bite, but his gaze seemed to bore into her. What if he tried to talk to her again? What should she say? She shoved a morsel of bread in her mouth, chewing deliberately slow.

"Uh, Miss Muffet," Lord Crawford began.

Elena closed her eyes and groaned internally. *Please be a reprehensible host and ignore me.*

"Would you care to borrow a book this morning?"

Elena wet her lips to erase any errant crumbs. Why did he have to mention her greatest weakness again? She glanced at him through her spectacles, careful to avoid his eyes, and nodded.

His smile showed his relief. "Very good. When you are finished eating, I will accompany you to the library."

Never had anyone watched her eat before—let alone a handsome, young earl. This would be more torturous than Bianca's methods.

"Please..." she said. "Go ahead and I shall join you shortly."

Lord Crawford's eyes widened, but he stood and excused himself. It wasn't like she *couldn't* talk, it was just that she didn't feel she was allowed to talk. It seemed ridiculous reasoning with him in her mind, but she wanted to explain herself. Perhaps with time, he would respect her silence without judging her as rude.

She ate quickly, not wanting to make Lord Crawford wait. With each step toward the library, she rehearsed her plan of action. Grab a book, thank Lord Crawford, and make an excuse to leave. The library door was open, and she could feel the books beckoning her in. Her father's library was part of his study, and she only went inside when he left town. The variety of books at home paled against the sheer number his lordship possessed.

"Ah, you have finished already?" Lord Crawford asked, closing a book in his hand and replacing it on the shelf. "I hope I did not rush you. My mother would not like it if her guest went hungry."

She supposed she should answer. "I wasn't very hungry." Nerves tended to render her a poor appetite. Visiting Banbury Castle was exciting and nerve-wracking all at once. Talking to Lord Crawford only heightened those emotions.

"Well then, what sort of books interest you?"

Elena glanced around. Extending her hand, she gently touched the spines on the row of books closest to her. She knew Lord Crawford awaited an answer, so she said softly, "I could be happy with a book of almost any genre."

"Really? No preference?"

"I . . . I do enjoy poetry, if well written." She turned away, as she remembered Lord Crawford liked poetry too. She could almost hear his voice reciting stanzas to Miss Bliss at their house party. Was he still heartbroken over losing Miss Bliss's hand to his younger brother?

"Do you have a favorite poet?"

"Milton." With her quick glance, she discovered Lord Crawford's amused smile.

"Let me guess, *Paradise Lost*?"

"Why, yes. Do you care for it?" Why was she making conversation? She knew Bianca's rules.

Lord Crawford took a step toward her. "I find its biblical retelling of Adam and Eve fascinating. I am merely eager to discover a woman's opinion on the poem."

She could not stop herself. Her opinion had never been sought after. "You think I should agree that a woman is responsible for the fall from paradise and, therefore, man should be viewed as above reproach?"

Lord Crawford seemed surprised by her again, but he only shrugged. "I am simply curious as to why it is your favorite. Milton was not exactly generous in the way he described the fairer sex."

She fingered the ridge on the top of a book near her. "I have not been educated on the theology behind the poem, only what I have learned at church and through my own studies." He patiently waited for her to finish. "The poem honors a man's right to choose. Almost all injustice stems from the desire to remove agency from man. Even a misuse of this power tends to limit it." Did he think her impertinent? She dared not risk another glance.

"I agree," he said.

His answer made her look without thinking, but she quickly focused on his cravat. "Truly?"

"Yes, but there is much in the poem I disagree with."

Her eyes widened behind her spectacles. She wanted to know his opinion more than she wanted to share her own. "I am sure your knowledge is far greater than my own," she whispered.

"I didn't mean to imply such a thing." Lord Crawford turned away from her to face the bookshelf. It placed him directly beside her, much closer than he was before. He thumbed through the books and pulled out a few, piling them in his arm. "Forgive me if I offended you. I just cannot fathom Adam choosing Eve over God. The idea does not sit well with me. The God I know would want Adam to be with Eve and would see the creation of a family as the first step of many leading to their redemption through Christ."

Elena repressed a smile. She was having her first enlightening conversation, and it was with a man . . . an earl even! The thought made her greedy enough to speak again. "I am not offended, Lord Crawford. In fact, I like your view on marriage better than Milton's." Now she had said too much. Heat rushed to her cheeks. "I . . . please, excuse me." She ducked her head and hurried from the room. Why did she have to ruin the moment by telling Lord Crawford she liked his view of marriage? How presumptuous could she be? And what would Bianca say if she found out? This was her second day here, and she had already broken so many rules. Elena twisted her fingers together all the way to her room. For all her painful efforts at discourse, she did not even have a book in hand to show for it.

Chapter 3

ONE WEEK DOWN, AND three weeks left with Miss Muffet. Anton entered the upstairs sitting room and sighed. It seemed too convenient to find Terrance, Gunther, and Mary on the balcony sipping lemonade at the exact time he needed to speak with them. Time to assess the situation and boost everyone's morale. He stepped closer, realizing they were already speaking about Miss Muffet.

"I tried to convince her to come with me the milliner's, but Miss Muffet informed me she does not wear ribbons—not even on her bonnets." Mary's brow cinched together. "Who does not wear ribbons?"

"I've never thought they complimented my complexion," Gunther said.

Terrance shook his head. "A shame. Ribbons might improve your appearance."

Mary gave them both a quelling look. "The point is, she turns down all my invitations."

Anton sank into a seat around the small table, and Mary poured him a glass of lemonade. "Surely, she must like one of us," he said. "We can't be that bad."

Terrance lifted his glass. "I did my best to befriend her when we met at Rosewood Park, remember? She has to want friends for any of our efforts to make a difference."

"Why is anyone worried?" Gunther asked. "The woman is content to stay in her room. I say, let her have her peace."

Anton shrugged. "I know she is a different sort of woman, but when have any of us shied from a challenge?" Anton took his role of hosting seriously, but he didn't want to be the lone entertainer.

Gunther's eyebrows danced. "A handsome, single earl like yourself shouldn't have any problems luring a girl from her room."

Anton recalled the spark of life Miss Muffet showed in the library the day she had arrived. Despite her soft voice, she had offered her opinions quite decisively. He'd been intrigued—not that he would admit that to anyone—and almost felt a sort of connection. Maybe a connection was a bit of a stretch, but no one else discussed literature with him. Her neck, on the other hand, he could not deny was fine indeed. He coughed into his hand. Regardless of his ridiculous thoughts, no one else seemed to be making any progress. He downed his lemonade. "Challenge accepted."

Gunther's eyes widened. "You were supposed to throw it back in my face. I don't want my best friend saddled with a hermit. She is not your equal in disposition."

"I'm not agreeing to marry her." The very idea made him laugh. "But I might be able to lure her from her room." Drat. The burden of earning the lady's regard was going to have to fall to him once more.

"Phew," Terrance said, from across the table. "We were worried about you for a moment."

"Everyone deserves a friend," he said.

Mary smiled at him. "I most heartily agree."

Anton pushed his seat back and stood. "No better time than the present, I suppose." He saluted the others and went to the library. He sifted through several titles before settling on the right one. Pulling the book from the shelf, he went to find Miss Muffet. He turned around and almost laughed at himself. There she was, sitting in the corner of the library on the little tuffet he often used as a footrest, her head buried in a book.

Her mousy brown hair was unusually thick with frizzy curls heavy in front to hide her face. He could not see her spectacles from this angle, but he noticed earlier that they were tinted and like a mask of glass, obscuring the color of her eyes. She was petite and almost childlike—especially when sitting on a stool.

Stepping closer, he accidentally spooked her, and she jumped from her position. Her book flew to the ground, and she backed up tight against the bookshelf. Anton's mouth dropped. Her spectacles were missing, and her eyes were large and doe-like. Her lashes, curled and profuse, framed two mesmerizing pools of blue.

They say the eyes are windows to the soul, and for a moment, Anton felt like he was staring into hers.

"Uh, er . . ." Anton was at a loss for words. This was a normal occurrence for him when facing a beautiful woman—just not one he expected to encounter with Miss Muffet.

"You startled me," she breathed.

Anton focused on her unflattering hair. "Forgive me. I stumbled upon a book I thought might interest you, but it seems you have found another."

Miss Muffet didn't smile, but she did relax her shoulders. "It's *Gulliver's Travels*."

Anton bent over and picked up the book. "So it is. How do you like it?"

"I like it very much. Might I ask what book you wanted to recommend?"

Anton held out *Gulliver's Travels* and the one he selected. "*Lyrical Ballads*—the most recent edition. Have you read it?"

"No, I am afraid my father keeps a small library." She eyed the book with eagerness.

"Please, take it. I particularly thought of "The Rime of the Ancient Mariner" by Coleridge. I hoped that if you liked poems with biblical symbolism, then this might appeal to you. There are other poems of worth in there as well."

She took both the books and pulled them to her chest. "Thank you."

Anton stared at her eyes again for a moment. He had her attention, so it seemed silly to let her escape back into a book. This was his chance to get to know her better and help her feel at ease at Banbury Castle.

"Do you play chess?"

She batted her long eyelashes and whispered, "A little."

"Good. You must play opposite me." His expression turned teasing. "It's practically your duty as a houseguest."

"Very well." She did not seem thrilled with the idea, but when he waved her toward the small rectangular table under the window, she followed.

Once they were seated, Anton urged Miss Muffet to make the first move. After several quick turns, assuring they were well into the game, Anton asked, "I, uh, noticed you are not wearing your spectacles. You must not need them to see the game pieces."

Miss Muffet cheek's flushed. "Oh, yes, I can see the game well enough. I did not realize I had forgotten to put them on."

"You must have fairly good eyesight. I assumed you were dependent upon them."

Miss Muffet didn't answer him but acted as if her next move required her utmost attention. He switched to a new line of questions. "What other sorts of pastimes do you enjoy outside of reading?"

She lifted her large eyes to meet his for less than a breath. "I like chess."

He couldn't help himself; he grinned. "I'm glad. You are good too. We might have to make this a regular activity while you are at Banbury."

"I . . . I should like that."

So, chess and books—two things he loved as well. "What else do you enjoy?"

Miss Muffet looked at the window and then once more at him. "Junket pudding."

She said it so quietly, he almost missed it. "Ah, so you have a sweet tooth." Her lips twitched, and she nearly smiled, he was sure of it. It might take a few more chess sessions, but he was determined to crack her. "I, too, love curds and whey. Is it a family favorite? Or, should I not ask about your family? It must be hard for you to be parted from them."

"You ask a great deal of questions, Lord Crawford."

For such a shy person, she delivered her quip without any sort of hesitation. He chuckled. "Why not ask me a question then? Anything, anything at all."

Miss Muffet wrinkled her petite nose as she thought. After a long moment, she whispered her question. "What do you enjoy?"

"This," Anton said, surprising both of them. After a moment he added, "Does that count?"

"What else?"

"I like spending time with my family, my dog, or my books. I'm not the most exciting person, I daresay."

"How long have you been the earl?" She asked the question so quickly; it was clearly not a thought-over question. He was glad she was letting down her guard.

"Two years. My father passed very suddenly, and sometimes I forget he is gone. I enjoy walking in his footsteps, but I am not nearly as dignified. Of course, he did not have my brother and Mr. Gunther as his closest friends. I am obligated to harass them in very childish ways, when the situation calls for it."

The corner of her mouth pulled up into a half-smile.

He wanted to cheer! An almost-smile. Not bad for someone who was generally too serious himself and usually stumbled all over himself when in the company of a lady. However, this was altogether different since this was only Miss Muffet.

"Any more questions?"

Miss Muffet scrutinized him for a moment. "Why are you doing this?"

"Doing what?"

"Being so kind to me."

Anton couldn't explain how his mother expected it, and everyone else in the house was far too involved in their own lives. Besides, no one else would likely understand the creature in front of him anyway. He had barely scratched the surface himself. "There is nothing wrong with being nice. Unless I am bothering you."

"No. I . . . I simply haven't been deserving of it."

Anton moved another pawn. "Everyone deserves kindness."

Miss Muffet did not argue, but there was a sadness in her expression—almost as if she did not believe the golden rule applied to herself. How very odd. Why would she think she was not worthy of kindness?

This sudden revelation made him want to try harder. Tomorrow's busy schedule seemed to fade away as he formulated how to prove to Miss Muffet that she mattered to the world. Gunther and Terrance would likely tease him that the little Miss Muffet had captured his fancy. It certainly wasn't a love project, but she had his full attention. Somewhere beneath her mop of hair and spectacles was a woman in need of tender care.

Chapter 4

MISS MUFFET STOOD IN front of her dressing table mirror examining herself. Had she imagined the way Lord Crawford had looked at her? For a moment, she thought she saw some sort of appreciation in his eyes. She pulled at her shapeless, brown day gown. Bianca selected all her clothes—the uglier the better. What Elena wouldn't give to wear something else today. She pushed back her ratted curls in front, cringing at the hairstyle Bianca had forced her to adopt.

Of course, Bianca wasn't watching now. Elena *could* be a different person here. The idea sounded enticing and intimidating. What would be her punishment should Bianca find out? Elena shivered at the thought. She needed to stick to her original plan and bide her time until Bianca married. There was no need to cause additional strife at home—a place where relations were already strained.

But Bianca did not need to know *everything* about her visit. Elena sighed and took her spectacles off. She set them on her dressing table in a small act of rebellion. Today she would forget them on purpose. Leaving her bedroom, she made her way down to the breakfast hall.

Each nook she passed possessed either some sort of historical relic or a vase of fresh flowers. When she pushed open the dining room door, she half-hoped to find Lord Crawford alone again.

Instead, she discovered Lady Mary and the countess.

"Good morning," Lady Crawford said, hurrying over to greet her.

Elena was so used to not responding, she nearly forgot to return the greeting. "Oh, good morning."

Lady Crawford paused, clearly surprised that Elena had spoken. Flustered by her own ineptness, Elena ducked her head and filled her plate. She took a seat opposite Lady Mary. Lady Mary caught her eye and gave her a wide smile—one Elena hardly deserved.

"Are you enjoying Banbury?" Lady Mary asked her. "I do hope you aren't homesick."

"I . . . I like it very much here." She forced herself to meet Lady Mary's eyes. She was fighting an internal battle of how much she should interact with the family. If she was too nice, Bianca would find some way to pit them against Elena when her stay at Banbury ended.

Lady Mary's smile widened. "Truly?"

Elena nodded. Who wouldn't enjoy staying in a real castle filled to the brim with history?

"What would you like to do today?" Lady Crawford asked, settling into the seat at the head of the table.

Bianca had trained Elena to always refuse invitations. "I will likely just read. Your library is quite extensive."

Lady Crawford gave her daughter an encouraging look.

"Oh," Lady Mary said, her eyes darting back and forth between Elena and Lady Crawford. "I was hoping you would come sketch with me in the garden."

Elena pinched her lips together. "I am not very accomplished."

Mary's smile drooped—the one she had willingly given Elena.

"Perhaps I could observe you?" The words slipped out of Elena's mouth. She twisted the napkin in her lap, hoping she would not regret them. "I could use the fresh air."

Lady Mary seemed satisfied. "Wonderful. While you gather your bonnet, I can collect my sketch pad."

Elena's fingers shook from her small act of bravery, but a wave of anticipation squelched the anxiety forming. What would it be like to have a friend? Was this what it felt like? She finished her last few bites and then retrieved her bonnet and shawl from her room. Lady Mary met her at the bottom of the stairs and led her around the back of the castle keep. They walked at a leisurely pace through the courtyard to a gate in the outer wall. To the left lay a large garden, surrounded by an oval gravel path with a second path running through its center.

"The skies are perfect for drawing, aren't they?" Lady Mary gave a delighted sigh and directed them to a bench near the stone wall and immediately sat and began sketching a fully bloomed rose.

"Do you care for roses?" Lady Mary asked, pausing her work.

Elena nodded. "Do . . . do you only draw flowers?" She over thought her question, worried Lady Mary would find her annoying for interrupting her artistic momentum.

"I love to draw still life, but I am partial to nature." Lady Mary pushed her dark curls away from her face and deftly moved her pencil across the page. "I do not care for painting, but sketching soothes me."

"You do it well." It felt good to compliment Lady Mary without any fear of repercussions. Elena had forgotten how nice it was to be herself. She craved it—yearned for it.

"Oh, thank you. Blake taught me. That is, Mr. Gunther, my intended. We grew up together, you know. When we were children, he couldn't stand the injustice I did to the people I drew. I made stick people without necks. It was quite abhorrent to him."

Elena nearly laughed. Lady Mary seemed like the perfect match for Mr. Gunther. He had joined them several nights for dinner, and she felt she knew them both through her quiet observations. When she had met Mr. Gunther at the same house party where she met Lord Crawford and Mr. Hastings, he had seemed like a supercilious dandy. Here, Lady Mary teased and harassed him and kept him in his place. Their relationship was nothing like Elena had ever seen before.

After a while, Elena stood to stretch her back and to walk through the carefully manicured garden. Sitting with Lady Mary wasn't the same as being in the company of her brother, and she felt restless. Elena didn't mean to wander far, but the grounds were extensive and beautiful. There was an orchard with rows of trees laden with nearly ripe apples and yellow-green pears just beyond the garden, and the long rows of trees beckoned to her.

She had nearly reached the other end of the orchard which bordered a meadow, when a nudge at the back of her skirt caused her to turn. A white collie with beautiful caramel patches jumped up on her skirt in a friendly, curious manner. Elena laughed softly and scratched his ears. Collies were working dogs for shepherds or farmers, and this one must have wandered off.

"You're a sweet one. Will you be my friend? Dogs are much safer company than people." She looked around for a stick to throw but didn't see one right away. "Come along, we shall find you something to play with." A few feet farther, beneath the shade of an apple tree, she found what she had been looking for. She threw the stick and watched the dog chase after it. They repeated the action a few times until the collie decided he did not want to give up the stick.

"You silly dog. Don't you want to play?"

"Is Patches bothering you?"

Elena turned to find Lord Crawford walking toward her. "Not at all. Do you know this dog?"

"Yes, he's mine. I wondered where he had gone."

Her brow pinched. How is it that a refined earl had chosen a collie for a pet? "Forgive me, I did not know." She remembered how he had said playing with his dog was one of his favorite pastimes.

"I don't mind if you spend time with him," Anton explained. "I would choose to be with a handsome woman over me. I can hardly blame him."

Elena ducked her head, her cheeks heating. Did he really think she was handsome? Surely, he was teasing her.

He stooped over and took the stick the dog would not give up for her. Then Lord Crawford tossed it in the distance, and the dog took off running. "What do you think of the gardens?"

"They are lovely." Her voice emerged soft and reverent. "But I must admit, I like the orchard and the open space even more."

"I am the same way. I like to wander out here and clear my head." He tossed her an easy smile, and she couldn't look away.

"You are truly fortunate to have such privacy." The desire for another conversation with this man overwhelmed her. How wonderful it was to be able to speak to someone without measuring each word and phrase.

"What is your estate like?" Lord Crawford asked.

She glanced around her. "It's a fine piece of land, not as large as this, nor as beautiful."

"I hope you take advantage of the yard while you are here. I know I am partial, but I haven't found a prettier spot in all of England."

"I thank you."

Lord Crawford stood and brushed off his breeches. "Care to walk with me?"

Elena hesitated, so Lord Crawford stuck out his arm, urging her to accept. With a burst of courage, Elena rested her hand on his arm. For a moment, she wondered if she was dreaming. It felt like a game of pretend—walking arm-in-arm through a green orchard with a handsome earl. He discussed literature with her and took the time to actually listen. He shared about his childhood, and didn't press when she did not share many details about hers. He was exactly who she needed him to be.

This moment was worth a hundred punishments.

After they returned to the spot at the edge of the orchard where they had met not a half hour before, she was ready to inquire about a topic burning in her mind. "Might I ask a question of you, Lord Crawford?"

"Didn't I give you permission to ask me questions while we played chess?"

She smiled. "Indeed, you did. Have you ever fought with your siblings?"

"Doesn't everyone?"

"I am sure you are right. It is only that I imagined you would resent your brother for his engagement to Miss Bliss, and yet, you seem so close."

"It was not an easy thing to get over, but Terrance is my brother. I cannot separate him from his heart. They are one and the same."

"Do you feel a family should always be united?"

Lord Crawford's silence lasted only a few steps. "None of us are identical spirits, but our goal can be the same. Don't you agree?"

"I don't know. I think sometimes they can be too different, thus preventing any opportunity for a common goal."

Lord Crawford shrugged. "I see such situations in society, but surely family is the one exception. A few sacrifices and compromises can go a long way."

Sacrifices. She knew much of that word.

Patches approached her, and she took the opportunity to change the subject. "Look how your dog comes to me as if he has known me all his life." Elena opened her free hand for the dog to lick. "If only everyone was as amiable as he is."

He stared at his animal for a moment. "Yes, I've never seen him take to a stranger so quickly."

Elena could almost say as much for herself. She had never taken to a stranger so quickly, but Lord Crawford might be the one exception. But how many days could she keep pretending that Bianca would not learn of their every interaction?

Chapter 5

Anton tried not to look Miss Muffet's way at dinner. Had she changed her hair, or was it just him? His self-control broke, and he stole a glance. Yes, there was considerably less of a frizzy mop around her face. The curls were tame and orderly, and the spectacles were missing again. She was far lovelier than before. In fact, he wondered why he had ever thought her common.

He took a bite of pheasant and a swig of his drink to wash it down. Mary and Gunther were arguing about who knew Terrance better and, instead of joining in, Anton was still reeling over thoughts of Miss Muffet.

She was supposed to be shy, but their conversation was progressively easier each time they spoke. And now she had changed her appearance? Something odd was going on. He felt duped for some reason. He wasn't supposed to enjoy getting to know her. He loved stimulating conversation, and Miss Muffet got his mind turning. She had asked him earlier what steps the House of Lords would take with the recent declaration of war against France and the Irish Rebellion.

Women in their station loathed political conversation, but he had been thinking of the very topic all morning. She couldn't have known. He'd told no one. Still, it seemed too strange.

"Hurry with the port so we might play charades." Mary dropped her napkin on the table and stuck her arm out for Miss Muffet. She accepted, and the two of them walked out together. Another oddity. He'd not expected to see them leave the dining room, like real friends. When had that happened?

When the women were gone, Terrance nudged him. "Where have you been all evening?"

Anton shrugged. He was in a pensive mood.

Gunther cleared his throat. "Look, Mary and I will take another turn with Miss Muffet tomorrow. You needn't feel so burdened by this. We know you are busy."

"Nonsense," Anton said, much too quickly. He wanted to spend time with Miss Muffet. That is what scared him. "It's my duty, and I won't shirk it. Thank you, though. I promise to let you know if it is too much."

Terrance smiled. "And this is why you are the earl and not me. You're a better man than Gunther and I could ever hope to be."

"Leave me out of this," Gunther said. "I should like to think I am as good as Anton."

Anton chuckled, feeling a bit lighter. "We shall see after a game of charades. You know I am the reigning champion."

The three men walked the short distance from the dining room to the drawing room and made themselves comfortable in the semicircle of seating. Anton's place next to Miss Muffet was purely by coincidence, as it was the last open seat since his mother's embroidery basket and sewing things took up half of a sofa. After he sat down, he realized it was too dark for his mother to sew and grew suspicious again.

Mary stood. "Let's divide into teams. Mother, you shall have to play. Blake, mother, and I will be on a team since we are sitting on this side of the room, and the rest of you shall be on the other team. I will go first. I have thought of just the thing."

"And likely told Mr. Gunther beforehand," Terrance said. "I think he and I should trade places to make this fair."

Mary huffed. "Very well. If you insist. But only because I know you desire to be on the more superb team and not because I have any intention of cheating."

The tiniest giggle erupted from Miss Muffet. Anton turned his head to see. Not even a smile graced her lips. Surely, he had imagined it.

"This is a person." Mary strutted across the room and pretended to fluff the front of her hair.

"Easy, it's me," Gunther said, before sitting up straight with a look of disgust. "Wait, are you mocking me? I thought you said you loved me."

Elena giggled again, and this time Anton caught her small smile. He laughed too. "You aren't on her team anymore, Gunther, remember?"

Gunther groaned.

Terrance shook his head. "Mary, you know most of the world plays this game very differently than you do. They act out every syllable in a line of phrases and create challenging riddles."

"The old way is stuffy," Mary argued. "Besides, I was only getting us excited about playing. It is all about acting now. Each team acts out a phrase or word. We can be as elaborate as we want with costumes and props. It's all quite exciting."

"Can we play a simplified version?" Anton asked. Mary's version could extend over several nights. "How about the teams all act out together, but they do it without costumes or props."

"You are eliminating half the excitement," Mary whined.

"We can go first, dear," Gunther said. "Just to show you how charming we can make this game."

"Let's convene to the dining room to discuss our part," Anton suggested. He extended a hand to Miss Muffet and helped her up from her seat. Once the door was shut behind them, Anton turned to his teammates, "Any brilliant suggestions?"

Miss Muffet's soft voice broke through the silence. "I have an easy idea since you seem intent on keeping this simple."

Anton had not expected her to be eager to play. She clasped her hands in front of her, as if she too did not expect her ready answer. His eyes took in her dress tonight—an orangish-brown that was not the least flattering. Not that it mattered to Anton. It was nice to have an excuse to look at her while she spoke instead of stealing glances.

"Simple sounds perfect," Gunther replied. "But we must draw it out a bit to satisfy Mary."

"What about a bluestocking?" Miss Muffet asked. "Three syllables but the parts to the word would make it simple to act out."

Anton nodded. "I like it. We could act out some sort of dyeing of cloth for blue."

"Yes," Gunther said. "You put out your arms in a circle, and Miss Muffet will make a dipping action into the vat."

"And what will you be doing, Gunther?"

"I will be a blue cloud, dancing rain on you."

Anton raised a brow. "Very original of you."

"I thought so."

"Very well," Anton said. "What about stocking?"

"We could pretend to knit and then point to our feet," Gunther answered. "You really can't complicate that one."

Miss Muffet pinched her lips to keep from laughing. Anton wanted to see her smile again, but how often could he justify looking at her? "All right," he said, directing his gaze to Gunther. "The third scene, we should have Miss Muffet hold a book and then stand on top of us. Just to give the right dramatic effect."

The giggle finally came out. He caught her alluring smile, and his whole body seemed to take note.

"What do you think of our ideas?" he asked her.

"I like the idea very much. Are we practicing this?"

"Heavens, no." Gunther shook his head. "Only amateurs rehearse."

Anton needed space to think over his reactions to her, so he took a deliberate step back and said, "Practicing detracts from the flair of spontaneity."

"So, we are to be three court jesters?" Miss Muffet asked.

"Exactly," Anton replied.

"Then please," Miss Muffet said in a soft but bold voice, "lead the way. Our audience awaits."

Anton blinked away his surprise at her sudden authoritative tone and extended his arm to give her permission to walk ahead of them.

Gunther jumped in line after Miss Muffet and turned to give Anton a curious look. Then he pointed to Miss Muffet and quirked his brow in question.

Shrugging, Anton followed them into the drawing room. This was not the time to explain the strangeness that was Miss Muffet. Indeed, he could not wait to see what she would do or say next.

Chapter 6

Elena had never been allowed to participate in charades before. The very idea made her giddy. This morning, she had committed to keeping herself aloof, but now she could barely remember her reasoning. It was hard to always watch from the side and never let herself experience any joy. This was a small group, and they acted as if they wanted her. When would another moment like this come around?

Her team stepped into the drawing room to find Mr. Hadley assisting two footmen with hanging a rope and some blankets to resemble stage curtains.

"What do you think?" Lady Mary asked, looking directly at Elena.

"It's charming!"

"See, Terrance," Lady Mary said to her brother. "I told you it was just the thing."

Terrance stepped back to admire his handywork. "I am more interested in whether or not the production will be entertaining enough to deserve a backdrop, but I am impressed with how we managed to secure this."

"Prepare to be thoroughly diverted," Lord Crawford said. "Gunther will likely hurt himself, but Miss Muffet and I will deliver an enthralling performance."

"Go ahead then," Lady Crawford said, laughing at her children. "Some of us aren't as young as we used to be and can't stay up for all hours."

Mr. Gunther, Lord Crawford, and Elena put themselves behind the curtain and assumed the first position. Lord Crawford squatted and put out his arms for their imaginary vat of dye. Mr. Gunther opened the curtains, and Elena held up three fingers to signify the number of syllables. Then she bent over to pick up a pretend bolt of cloth. But as she moved to dip it into Lord Crawford's arms, she felt a small push from behind. Since she was already leaning forward, she fell headfirst against Lord Crawford.

She squeaked in surprise. Lord Crawford managed to open his arms to catch her, but his perch on his toes did not lend for a steady base. He toppled over with Elena sprawling on top of him.

Their small audience laughed as if this was part of their act. Lord Crawford lifted her up by her shoulders, and their eyes connected. He froze, his face a mixture of astonishment and fascination. Mortified, she pulled away and managed to get back on her feet, all while Mr. Gunther danced rain around them.

"Stop!" Mary said, holding her stomach from too much laughter. "Blake, I cannot watch you another moment. I'm afraid for our future children."

This caused Elena to snort with laughter and, before she knew it, her and Lord Crawford were laughing at Mr. Gunther's ridiculousness too. Lord Crawford caught her eye and grinned just as the curtain closed.

"I am so sorry," Elena whispered to Lord Crawford.

Lord Crawford shrugged, truly more amused than upset. "The show must go on. What now? Darning stockings?"

Mr. Gunther nodded. "Prepare to be amazed. My knitting skills are my best-kept secret." No one would believe Mr. Gunther could knit—his broad shoulders, strong masculine presence, and flapping mouth made the idea more ridiculous. He was the least serious person Elena had ever met.

She turned to share her amusement with Lord Crawford, who winked at her. She had heard only scandalous things about what it meant when a man winked at a woman, but from Lord Crawford, it felt like a shared secret.

Mr. Gunther pulled open the curtain, and the three of them started mimicking the process of knitting. They stood in a line starting with Mr. Gunther, Lord Crawford in the middle, and Elena on the end. Lord Crawford lifted up one leg and pointed to his foot. Then he began hopping on one foot behind their little line until he was behind Mr. Gunther. Out of the corner of her eye, Elena saw Lord Crawford take his raised foot and kick Mr. Gunther in the backside.

Elena gasped as Mr. Gunther dove forward. So, this was the reason for Lord Crawford's wink. Mr. Gunther did not land on his face but managed to catch his footing. He turned to scowl at Lord Crawford right as Lord Crawford closed the curtains. Holding her stomach now, Elena did her best to get her giggles under control.

She heard Terrance say from the other side of the curtain, "I am not sure these scenes are painting a very clear picture for me."

Lady Mary's voice responded, "Yes, they are either very good actors or the very worst."

Mr. Gunther popped through the curtain to their side but bowed to the audience as he did.

"Perhaps we should have rehearsed," Mr. Gunther said. "There have been one or two surprises, I daresay. Already, I wonder what will happen in scene three. As a coauthor to this whole arrangement, I shouldn't wonder at the ending."

Lord Crawford cleared his throat and managed a straight face. "This act will go on without a hitch. Gunther, open the curtain and then prostrate yourself on the ground."

Mr. Gunther raised an eyebrow. "Such a position makes me feel quite vulnerable."

"Oh, go on," Lord Crawford said. "Miss Muffet, might you make your hands into the shape of a book?"

Elena complied and without further ado, Lord Crawford reached over and scooped her into his arms. She gasped and her hands split apart and clasped Lord Crawford around the neck.

"Miss Muffet, I know it must be tempting to embrace me, but you must remember we are in the middle of a performance."

His words were playful, and she had to bite her lip to keep from laughing again. She released him and put her hands together just as Mr. Gunther opened the curtain. Mr. Gunther dropped to the ground, and Lord Crawford put one foot on his back. A beat later, he lifted Elena up, so she nearly sat on one shoulder. Another gasp emitted from her mouth, and she had to steady herself with one hand on Lord Crawford's head. As soon as she gained her balance, she put her hands back into position.

They held their pose for a few counts, and then Lord Crawford lowered her back into his arms and stepped off of Gunther. Gunther jumped up and closed the curtain, cutting off their audience but not the sound of their clapping.

Lord Crawford kept Elena in his arms for a moment and studied her. "You are very light, Miss Muffet. I should think I could carry you all night."

Miss Muffet suddenly had an urge to push back a tuft of black hair on his forehead—to touch his face. In one exhale, her heart seemed to leave her in a single breath. The feelings she'd saved for a future hope now belonged to him. This was not the time, nor the man, she thought she would fall in love with. He leisurely set her on her feet, his arm slow to leave her back. All the while, his eyes remained on her.

Did he realize what had happened inside of her just now? This was supposed to be a silly game, but her heart felt lighter than she could ever remember, and it was all because of him.

They followed Mr. Gunther out behind the curtain to return to their prospective seats and hear the guesses of the others. Elena's smile could not be hidden now. There was no adopting a mask of pretense. Not tonight.

"I would like to guess the answer," Lady Crawford said, her eyes glinting with triumph.

"I should like to hear this," Mr. Gunther said as an aside to Lord Crawford.

Lady Crawford put her hands together and placed the tips of her fingers to her lips. "Falling, dressing, praying. It has to be true love! First, the awkwardness of new love. The second scene, they can't quite dress themselves, which clearly demonstrates how love sneaks up on us. Never is one quite prepared. Then last, the bride sends a prayer to heaven on behalf of her new love. Anton lifted his bride up, showing he will always put her before every other man." She smiled rather triumphantly. "It was quite symbolic when you stepped on Mr. Gunther. I am duly impressed."

Elena scrunched her forehead. That was not the conclusion they intended, but Lady Crawford's assumption nearly paralleled Elena's feelings. Had her emotions been so obvious that everyone had guessed them? She glanced over to see Lord Crawford's jaw slack.

"Is that the answer?" Mary asked. "I admit to being vastly entertained, but I cannot fathom what it was all about."

Terrance shook his head. "I am baffled, myself. Mother's guess is as good as any."

Mr. Gunther scratched his head. "I see Anton got his deep thinking from his mother. And I would have to agree with her conclusion."

"Agree with her?" Lord Crawford laughed. "You know what the true answer is. We stumped them."

"I saw what they saw," Mr. Gunther argued. "I think this means it's the other team's turn. It will be impossible to outshine us, but do try."

Heat flooded Elena's cheeks. Were they laughing at her or the silly game? And what of Lord Crawford? She did not want to put him in an uncomfortable position. Not that she hadn't already been in his arms twice in one night.

"Wait!" Lord Crawford said. "Doesn't anyone want to know the real answer?" The other three had already stood.

"Tell us later," Mr. Hadley said. "I am in need of a good night's sleep. Miss Bliss arrives in two days, and I want to get a few things settled in the morning."

"Yes, we can continue the game tomorrow," Lady Crawford said, stifling a yawn. "Mary, dear, please say goodnight and follow me up."

Everyone said goodnight, and Elena soon found herself in her room. Sitting on the edge of her bed, she realized she had discovered something new about herself. She enjoyed group games! She had always bowed out of invitations to play, knowing that it would please Bianca. She fell back on her bed and covered her eyes with her hands. Oh, but Lord Crawford did not like the insinuation of her as his feigned new bride. Her embarrassment quickly melted under the warm memory of being held by him. She shook her head against her quilt. She shouldn't ruin their new friendship by presuming Lord Crawford had feelings for her. Such a notion was beyond ridiculous. His temporary companionship was treasure enough.

Chapter 7

ANTON WANTED TO PRETEND nothing had changed after their game of charades, but then he would be lying to himself. Something had changed, and it drove him to his horse the next morning and into the countryside. His dog chased after him for a time but finally gave up when he realized Anton wasn't going to slow down.

All these ideas about Miss Muffet were figments of his imagination induced by a broken heart. Miss Bliss, the woman he really loved, was coming tomorrow. He waited for the heartbreak inside him to twist at his heart, but this time, he felt nothing. The curious absence of the perpetual ache made him slow his horse to a trot. Was he truly over Miss Bliss? Now that he thought on it more, the fervor of his emotions toward Miss Bliss had been lessening steadily since the house party.

It had been hard to accustom himself to the idea of his brother marrying the girl he had chosen for himself. He had agreed to be supportive and to bury his feelings. Was it possible to have buried them so deeply that they could no longer be found? He had woken this morning with thoughts of Miss Muffet on his mind—and her alone.

Wiping a bead of sweat from his brow, he sat back in his saddle. He must be delusional. The mousy, quiet little thing had stolen into his heart without him even realizing it.

But how could he care for someone he did not even know? She was entirely unpredictable. Last night her appearance improved—outside of her distasteful dress—and her charming smile made its debut. At first, she would not even look at him and his family, but now she managed to get along with his family. Indeed, she did so without taking offense by their ridiculousness or teasing.

Something was off. There was an inconsistency about her behavior he couldn't quite trust. It bothered him greatly that he was developing feelings for her when he could not foresee her actions. He needed to discover more about her.

Having a plan of action soothed his anxiety, and he turned his horse and headed home. Upon his return to the castle, he changed clothes and went in search of Miss Muffet. He stopped in the library, sure he would find her there, but the room was vacant. A little more exploring, and he discovered her with his mother and sister by the front door.

"You're sure you won't come?" Mary asked Miss Muffet, clasping her hands around Miss Muffet's. "I promise you would be most welcome."

"Your friends sound wonderful." Miss Muffet played with the fabric of her skirt. "I am not quite ready for such an outing, but I will try to prepare myself for next time."

"You take as long as you need," his mother said. "Miss Bliss will be here tomorrow, and I am sure a familiar face will be more comfortable than a stranger's."

"Thank you for understanding," Miss Muffet produced a small smile, barely visible from his position.

"Oh, Anton." Mother caught him listening and waved him over. "We are going to make a few house calls. Do see to any need our Miss Muffet has."

"Of course." Anton strode up alongside Miss Muffet, and they both said goodbye. He turned to Miss Muffet. "This might be the perfect opportunity to redeem myself in chess. Do you have a spare moment for a sore loser?"

Miss Muffet looked up at him with her large doe eyes and gave him a timid smile. He wondered how hard it was for her to make such an expression of happiness. What held her back?

"I happen to be free right now."

"Well then, shall we?" He put out his arm, and she took it. As they walked back toward the library, he congratulated himself for securing her all to himself.

"I wanted to tell you, I read the 'Rime of the Ancient Mariner' this morning." Her soft voice reminded him of the gentle coos of a dove.

Anton led her through the library door to the chair on the other side of the rectangular table. The chess game was already there like a piece of permanent décor. "What did you think of the poem?"

She sat down and crossed her arms in a comfortable position. "I am sure there are a great deal of translations as to its meaning, and I wanted the ending to resonate with me more." She straightened the chess pieces in front of her. "But I did like it. There are stanzas I cannot forget."

Anton wanted her to expound—wanted to see how her mind ticked. "Please, tell me. What part stood out to you?"

When her gaze met his, her posture and expression were open and not guarded as in past days. "When the mariner is forced to wear the albatross he killed on his neck, I could relate."

He studied her, wondering what sort of experiences could make her identify with the chilling poem. "How so?"

She began straightening the pieces once more. "We all have times where burdens rain down on us from every side. Some of us even have nightmarish sea monsters, keeping us riveted in our grief. I feel for the mariner, cursed as he was, and forced to watch all those horrors around him. Yet, fear kept him stuck in his situation—from being able to even whisper a prayer."

"Until the turning point."

She nodded. "That part was rushed and almost hidden. I'm not sure anything so awful could end so easily. That certainly hasn't been my experience. Yet somehow, he managed to feel some sort of affection for his enemy and could finally utter his prayer. I'm not sure how he could feel affection for anything so awful. I surely could not. Yet, the very act released the albatross, and it sank into the sea. In one quick stanza, his whole reality changed, and suddenly there was hope."

Anton watched her eyes light up with passion as she spoke. He loved finding parables in literature. "After all the horrors he sees, I think a breath of hope was all he needed. Does it change your perception or does it align with your previous methodology of thought?"

"I . . . I am not sure. The similarity to my own life was . . . uncanny."

"I would be interested in hearing more about the connection," he said, hoping she would confide in him.

She shrugged, walls building behind her eyes. "It is hardly worth mentioning. Let's start our game. I believe it is your turn to go first."

Anton stared hard at her for a moment longer. Though she was quite a puzzle to him, he enjoyed discussing literature with her. It was nice to share what he loved with someone. He looked down long enough to move a pawn. "If you should find yourself comfortable enough to share more with me, I hope you will find the courage to do so. I enjoy hearing your thoughts. In fact, I can see why you came up with the word bluestocking last night. Your intelligence does you credit."

Miss Muffet's cheeks pinked, and her attention became riveted on the chessboard.

"I'm sorry if I made you uncomfortable," he hedged. "I assure you, it was not my intention. I simply find your conversation most refreshing."

Miss Muffet lifted her gaze. "I am not used to expressing my thoughts. You are an adept listener, and I cannot help but prattle on."

"I have yet to hear you prattle." He moved another pawn when his turn came again. "Tell me, don't you share confidences with your sister? I assume you are close in age."

"You might say." Miss Muffet hesitated before moving her rook. "We are twins.

"Twins? I never would have guessed with your differing appearance. It must be hard to be away from her."

"On the contrary." Miss Muffet's soft voice was suddenly laced with derision. "I mean . . ." she took a moment to finish her sentence. "My sister is . . . well, she is Bianca. I cannot describe her. I am always in her shadow and content to be there."

Anton tried to process what she had said and guess at what she wasn't saying. He thought about her impression of the story he recommended. She said the mariner appreciated a form of life he had not before. Is that the part Miss Muffet thought resembled her own?

"Miss Muffet, do you hope your life will change when you return home?" Thunder and turf, he thought. That was only two weeks away.

"Change is inevitable, is it not? I can only hope the future has good things in store for me—hopefully, better than for the haunted mariner." She spoke the words readily, but he sensed an undercurrent of uneasiness when she spoke.

He wondered if he shared a little of himself with her, if she would do the same. "Change can be hard. I am still adjusting to life without my father. I have learned happiness largely depends on our perspective and whether we have the courage to allow ourselves to be happy."

Her gaze drifted to the window, fatigued by some hidden burden he could not see. "What if courage is not one's strong suit?"

"Ah," Anton said, capturing one of her pawns with his. "When playing cards, it is still possible to win with strategy, even without the trump suit. I think even a timid person as yourself has some tricks up her sleeve."

Miss Muffet's eyes shifted back to his, and the sparkle returned. "I didn't think so before. Perhaps with the proper motivation, I will perform better.

His brow rose. "What would motivate you?"

Miss Muffet stared at him for a moment. Then her lips curled up into a mischievous grin. "I have an idea, but it is of a private nature, and I dare not tell you. Now I must work on my strategy." She moved her knight into check position.

Blast. He hadn't seen that coming. "I doubt you will struggle there."

She gave a soft, musical laugh. "You would be surprised."

Undoubtedly.

Miss Muffet had captured his attention, and he could no longer doubt it. There was something to be said for a person to be aware of their own weaknesses and yet, eager to improve themselves. He found her personality refreshing. So many people he met were eager to prove they were the best, when in reality, they were hiding their flaws behind pretense. It wasn't just her modesty, but she had no ulterior motive to use his family for their rank or position. Their conversation—their time together—started because of circumstance but now had gradually turned into a genuine desire to know each other better.

Was this how it had happened for his siblings? It made him think of Terrence and then of Miss Bliss. The thought of his former *tendre* came and left without any care. Thoughts of Miss Muffet, however, were flooding through his mind with a vengeance he had never experienced before. He wanted to know her secrets and protect her from them.

Chapter 8

ELENA'S HANDS TREMBLED. SHE finished reading the letter that had just arrived for her and creased it shut. While her mother had penned most of the letter, the last few lines were from Bianca. *Take care not to act in any manner you may later regret. It would be a shame if anyone there was hurt as a consequence of your actions. Not everyone is as forgiving as I am. Farewell for now. I cannot wait to see you.*

No one else would think twice about such empty sentiments. Elena, however, knew Bianca's hidden meaning. When Elena returned, there would be no end to her punishments. Worse, Bianca might even hurt her new friends to hurt Elena even more.

She put a finger in her mouth and chewed her nail. Would Bianca really stoop to hurting Lord Crawford—an earl—if she discovered their friendship? She thought of the scissors Bianca had snipped her hair with, and the blood she had later found dried on her chest from Bianca's pointed fingernail. There was no doubt that Bianca had an unpredictable temper.

If Elena were to protect Lord Crawford, spending time together at all would have to be forbidden. Bianca would know otherwise. Elena would miss Lord Crawford—Anton. Mary always called her brother Anton, so Elena had begun to think of him that way. And while she did not have permission to drop Mary's title, she hoped by the end of her stay they would be good enough friends to do so in person.

She dropped her hand with frustration. It wasn't right for Bianca to ruin the last of her freedom. Even if she were to be a hermit in her room, Bianca was going to make her life miserable when she returned. Elena should continue to act as she pleased and not fret about Bianca's concealed threats. The decision would come with consequences, but she might never have the same opportunities again. When the inevitable time came to return home, she would have ample chance to worry then.

With a deep breath, Elena pushed her anxiety to the back of her mind. Leaving the privacy of her room, she went down the corridor to search for Mary. Mary had promised to teach Elena to sketch Banbury Castle so she might take home a small likeness of it. She walked toward the staircase when Mary turned a corner.

"I was just coming to fetch you," Mary said with her familiar wide smile. "Did you remember our drawing lesson?"

Elena nodded. "Am I late? I would dearly like to learn."

"Not at all. I have never taught anyone before, but I am eager to try."

Elena smiled too. "Shall we then?"

Mary linked arms with her. "I have everything ready beyond the gatehouse where we can have the best view of the castle."

Elena had never had another girl take her by the arm in such ready friendship, and the gesture suppressed the anxiety building inside of her. Miss Bliss would be arriving in a few hours, and Elena would surely be pushed to the shadows again, but right now it felt wonderful to be cared for.

Just as Mary had said, the servants placed a bench a short walking distance from the house, giving them the perfect angle to sketch. Golden sunlight peeked through the clouds, warming her face.

Mary handed Elena one of the two sketchbooks. "You seem to have grown more at ease with us, Miss Muffet. I'm so glad."

Elena ran her finger down the spine of her sketchbook. "It is kind of you to spare time for me when I know you could be with Mr. Gunther."

"I cannot be with him all the time. We would drive each other mad." Mary flipped her sketchbook open. "A man is wonderful for many reasons, but a woman needs the comfort and friendship of another woman. It is in our nature. We crave the companionship found in sisterhood."

Elena felt the same longing for companionship but had never realized how much until she'd been given a taste of it. "I've never really had a friend," she admitted. Her governesses had been genuinely kind, but they were still paid to be there for her.

Mary turned her knees toward Elena. "You and your sister must be close."

"Everyone assumes as much, but it isn't so. We are very different." Elena was not used to revealing so much of herself. Between all the information she shared with Mary and Anton, Elena suddenly felt very vulnerable.

Mary set the sketchbook on her lap with a firm plop. "Well, *we* are friends, are we not?"

The corner of Elena's lips pulled upward. "Yes, I'd like to think so."

"Perhaps we should drop formalities then. Will you just call me Mary?"

Elena could not hold back her smile. "Really? Then you must call me Elena."

"Elena is a beautiful name. I can already see your signature on your first sketch—Miss Elena Muffet." Mary made a flourish in the air with her hand. "What do you think?"

Elena giggled. "What a splendid idea—as long as the picture is worth claiming."

"Well said. We had better not waste any time then."

Mary spent the next hour walking Elena through the various lines of drawing the house, instructing where to shade and where to use less pressure. Elena's sketch was not as precise as Mary's, but it at least resembled Banbury.

A dog barked, and she turned to see Patches bounding toward them. Not far behind him was Anton. The dog raced straight to her and nuzzled against her leg. She rubbed his ears and looked up to see Anton's amusement. He glanced at their sketchbooks. "One would think I was in France, joining the artists painting Versailles."

"Hardly," Mary scoffed.

Anton looked over Elena's shoulder. "I didn't know you could draw, Miss Muffet."

"I can," Elena said, "as of today."

"You must have some ready talent then."

Mary leaned over to see better. "I was just about to say the same. I should ask Blake if he could offer any better advice. You are quite the natural."

Elena shook her head. "If you are both attempting to put me at ease here, I assure you, it is working. I promise to keep practicing my drawing, but only if you both cease complimenting me at once."

"Being overbearing is a family trait, I'm afraid," Mary laughed.

"The girls are worse than the boys," Anton clarified. "Except for Mother. She is an angel. My older sister Jillian is as vexing as Mary."

Mary sighed. "I cannot even argue with him."

A carriage turned up the drive, and Anton went rigid next to her. Elena bent her head to see what had caused such a reaction. The familiar crest alerted her at once. Miss Bliss was here. Disappointment balled in her stomach. Receiving attention from Anton had been wonderful, but she knew his intentions were friendly. It did not matter that he was everything she knew she wanted, for his heart belonged to another. No one who knew Miss Bliss would question why he felt as he did. Where she radiated light, Elena was meant for the shadows.

"Who could that be?" Mary set down her drawing things. "Oh! It has to be Miss Bliss! We have been introduced but once, and I am eager to know her better. Come," Mary reached for Elena's hand. "You must greet her with me."

Anton pushed back his jacket and set his hand on his waist, his eyes solemn. Elena could sense him watching the carriage, even after she looked away. As much as she was sad for herself, she hurt for him. He did not deserve to live with a broken heart.

The three of them walked back through the gate and across the courtyard to meet the carriage, which had pulled to a stop in front of the keep. A footman jumped down and opened the carriage door. Miss Bliss stepped out, her golden curls bouncing.

"Miss Muffet! Lady Mary!" Her smile was wide and genuine. She walked toward them and grabbed both of their hands. "It is so good to see you both!" She bent her head back and took in the overbearing, stone structure. "So, this is Banbury Castle."

"I hope you like it." Lady Mary glanced over her shoulder at her home. "It's intimidating on the outside, but I assure you that it feels like home on the inside. Terrance will be so happy to see you."

"And I him." Miss Bliss blushed and ducked her head momentarily. "Will you take me to him?"

The castle doors swung open, and Terrance emerged as though he had been heralded with trumpets. Elena had never seen his smile so wide. He skipped down the steps and jogged toward them. Miss Bliss dropped their hands in anticipation, and they stepped to give the couple room.

Terrance reached her, and without care for propriety, pulled Miss Bliss into his arms. "I was certain you were not coming until evening. I just happened to look out the window, and there you were." He pulled back and stared at his intended. "I've missed you, Sophia."

Miss Bliss sighed with happiness. "You cannot fathom how much I've missed you."

"Oh, but I can." Terrance pulled her against him again and kissed her.

"I need a fan," Mary said, waving her hand in front of her face. "I've never seen my brother like this."

Elena did something brave again. She linked arms with Mary. "Isn't it wonderful?"

Anton came and stood next to Elena. She tensed with concern for him. He cleared his throat loudly, and Terrance and Miss Bliss broke their kiss. Terrance didn't fully release his future bride, but kept her close as he looked over her head at his brother. "My apologies to everyone but myself."

Elena stole a glance at Anton, and caught his half-amused, half-annoyed expression. What did it mean?

"Lord Crawford," Miss Bliss turned in Terrance's arms, offering an awkward curtsy. "How do you do?"

Anton dipped his head in a quick bow. "I trust your journey was smooth?"

"Yes, thank you."

Terrance finally released Miss Bliss and scooped up her hand. "Enough of this proper speech. We are going to go find Mama and get you settled into a room. Are you hungry?"

"Famished," Miss Bliss said.

"Excellent, because as soon as I saw the carriage, I sent for tea and refreshments."

Mary put her head near Elena's. "Do you think we are invited?"

"No," Anton said, overhearing. "Tomorrow perhaps, but I think our love birds could use a few minutes without an audience."

There was not a hint of malice in his words. He was truly the best of brothers.

"That's a sweet thought, Anton." Mary gave Elena a quick smile. "My older brother is wiser than all of us when it comes to romance. I cannot wait to see him fawning over a girl."

Anton groaned and called for Patches. The pair strode away, and Elena had to force her eyes from following his handsome form. Mary was right. Anton would be the perfect suitor for someone. Was it wrong to wish to be that person?

Chapter 9

Chapter 9

Anton couldn't very well avoid dinner with the family. He dearly wanted to after seeing how affectionate Miss Bliss was with his brother, but he had no ready excuse. It hadn't hurt him to see it like he imagined, but it had been confusing. Now he found himself at the dinner table, sitting at the head of the table with Miss Bliss on his left, and he had to do his level best not to look at her. She was a rare beauty, but it was more awkward than anything.

"Lord Crawford."

Oh, why did she have to talk to him? "Yes?"

"Are you ready for another session of parliament?"

He feigned a smile. "I will be when it comes."

"My father will not put down his newspapers. I fear you shall be very busy next year."

"Anton is the same," Terrance said. "Except when he is challenged in chess by Miss Muffet."

Anton did not expect Terrance's comment, and he squirmed in his seat. He wasn't sure how he felt about Miss Bliss—or anyone else for that matter—knowing about his time with Miss Muffet. He glanced down the table to find Miss Muffet with her head down over her chicken fricassee with mushrooms—she seemed to have no intention of eating. He knew she did not care for public attention, and she was likely worried about Anton's response.

"Yes," he answered, his chest warming as he thought of their time together. "I have not found a better opponent than Miss Muffet. I have yet to beat her."

Miss Muffet looked up, and her doe eyes melted the walls he had spent the morning building around his heart. Miss Bliss might be a renowned beauty, but Miss Muffet was the one who stirred him inside. His posture relaxed and he smiled, this time without pretense.

He stabbed a mushroom with his fork. On its way to his mouth, he noticed Mama looking at him curiously. Drat. He did not need his family drawing conclusions before he was ready. He would need to be careful. It would be wise to completely understand his feelings this time. He was not the only one capable of having their heart broken. Forcing the mushroom into his mouth, he concentrated on chewing and eating. It felt like a safer course of action than thinking about the subject of romance. After all, there was a strong possibility that Miss Muffet might only be in his life for another two weeks.

Miss Bliss had been at Banbury Castle for three days now. They sat close in Mary's sitting room on the second floor and sipped their tea. Outside, a soft rain pelted against the windows. While the weather cast a gray hue over the room, it did not detract from their visit. Elena gazed over the gold rim of her cup at Miss Bliss. Despite her beauty, Miss Bliss was modest in her manners. Elena envied her easy nature around the family. There were no haughty airs like Bianca and the many other debutantes Elena had met, just an ample amount of kindness.

When Elena had met Miss Bliss at Rosewood Park, Elena had not cared one bit about knowing her. She had been intent on avoiding Bianca and anything her sister deemed as special. Here at Banbury, Elena had adopted a different mindset. Part of her worried that Mary would cast her aside for Miss Bliss, but the other part wanted to believe she could make another friend.

"Miss Bliss," Mary's voice took on a note of excitement. "What do you think of a picnic?"

"Please, you must call me Sophia now. We are to be family, are we not?" Sophia turned to Elena. "You, too. We have been thrown in each other's company often this summer, and we ought to put aside niceties."

Elena blushed at the sweet gesture. "I should like that. Please, call me Elena."

"I would enjoy nothing better. Now let's hear more about this idea for a picnic."

"I thought it would be a splendid way to celebrate the arrival of your parents and grandmother," Mary explained, "and perhaps introduce them to some of our neighbors. Mama approved, but we both thought it best to ask your family's preference first."

Sophia seemed pleased. "How kind of you to think of them. I would like to meet a few of the families in the neighborhood. My parents always enjoy making new acquaintances, but my grandmother will likely prefer to stay at the castle. Will it be too much trouble with the wedding plans? I should not like to burden the household staff."

"My mother has employed a few temporary staff members to accommodate the extra guests. It won't be any trouble at all."

"What about you, Elena? Do you enjoy picnics?"

Elena had been listening quietly and hardly expected to be included in the decision. "A picnic sounds lovely."

They both looked at her as if expecting her to say more; but surely, they did not care to hear of past ways her sister had made picnics less than enjoyable for her. Thankfully, the opportunity to be with her new friends on an outing surpassed the displeasure of her memories.

"Wonderful!" Mary clapped her hands together. The teacup on her lap wobbled, and she quickly moved to balance it. "Oh dear. My eagerness for the picnic is not worth burning my legs. Perhaps we had better talk of something else. I know! Let's compare wedding plans, Sophia. I have been anxious to learn what you and Terrance have planned."

Elena shifted in her seat. She would be gone before either wedding ceremony, and for that reason, it always made her uncomfortable to listen to wedding preparations. They were quiet affairs, so it shouldn't matter that she was not invited. Perhaps it was because she had so little opportunity to attend weddings and even wondered if she would ever have one herself.

"Mary," a voice called from the door. They all turned to see Anton on the threshold. "I daresay the topic of Terrance's wedding trip is none of your business."

Mary stuck her tongue out at her brother, and Elena had to bite her lip to keep from smiling.

"At least spare Miss Muffet."

Mary pushed her breath out and made a noise of annoyance. "You think she would prefer to play chess with you over spending time with us?"

Elena did not want to admit that, despite how close the competition would be, Anton would win every time. Chess or not.

"I am sure I could provide some riveting, intellectual conversation for our little bluestocking." He looked at her and grinned.

Heat rushed to her cheeks without her permission.

"You are embarrassing her!" Mary chided. "Go and find Terrance or Blake. We have commandeered this room for the ladies only."

"Fine, but I should like to request Miss Muffet's presence for at least a few moments. I have found something of interest for her."

Elena stood rather quickly, before Mary could think of another reason she should stay. She followed him down the staircase toward the library. It was chilly, likely from the drop in temperature because of the rain. The room sat empty except for a servant girl who coaxed a fire in the grate.

"Are you cold?" Anton must have followed her gaze or noticed the way she was hugging herself.

"I forgot my shawl in Mary's sitting room."

He frowned and turned to the maid. "Sarah, might you fetch Miss Muffet's shawl?"

"Yes, your lordship." She dipped a curtsy and hurried from the room.

"Come sit by the fire. In a few moments the room should warm up." He put his hand on the small of her back and gently led her to a chair by the fire. She sat down, and he grabbed a chair from the table and pulled it opposite her. Sarah entered only a moment later with her shawl.

"Thank you." Elena draped the coal-colored wool over her shoulders. "It isn't dainty like many a lady's, but I made this for the warmth."

"You made that?" He seemed impressed.

"Yes, I enjoy all sorts of needlework—knitting, crocheting, and even lacework."

"I knew you were hiding more secrets."

She only carried one real secret. Would she ever be able to tell him about her sister? Her gaze lifted to Anton's. "You wanted to speak to me about something?"

"Not really." Anton's expression turned sheepish. "I only cared to spare you the awkward wedding talk."

Elena's lips quirked. "It does get a tad excessive at times."

"At times? I haven't seen either of them speak of anything else when together."

She laughed. "I don't mind terribly."

"No? Well then, you are more patient than I."

Elena wondered if it was because of his feelings for Sophia or his bachelor status that made him feel this way. "Will you not be the same when you are engaged to be married?"

Their eyes met. He stared at her for a moment, and she couldn't look away like she normally did. What was he thinking?

"No doubt I will be just as in love. But I imagine I will keep most of my feelings close to my heart rather than share them."

"Your stance does you credit."

"You think so?" His gaze intensified on her face, warming every feature.

She had to look away to form a coherent answer. "To keep your feelings private demonstrates a level of sacredness."

He casually leaned over the arm of his chair toward her, drawing her gaze once more. "I've never thought of it that way, but it perfectly puts to words my take on the matter."

She dug her hands into the weave of her shawl, happy to know that once more they shared the same opinion.

"What would you be like?" Anton asked. "If you were engaged."

She shrugged. "Blissfully, ecstatically happy. If I loved him, of course."

Anton smiled. "And would you want to tell the whole world?"

"I think I would burst with desire to tell, but I rarely trust my deepest thoughts with anyone."

"Trust is important to any relationship. When I first met you, I thought you were merely shy. Now I wonder if you are just more guarded."

"I am guilty of both. Smaller groups are easier for me. And I must say, being here at Banbury has allowed me to be more open than ever before."

"Then you are growing more trusting of us?"

She shook her head, amused. "If I answer yes, you will surely keep prying at all my dark secrets."

Anton stretched his legs out in front of him and leaned back in his chair. "Dark secrets? This I must hear."

She shook her head again. "The only thing I have to recommend of myself is the air of mystery I carry about my person."

Instead of laughing like she thought he would, his lips drooped into a frown.

"Why would you think that? You possess many exceptional qualities. You do not simper and play games like other debutantes. That alone raises you in my book. You are intelligent, patient—especially with my family—and a terribly good listener. Look at me spouting on and on. You never even seem remotely bored with my conversation when I know I am the least entertaining person in this house."

"How can you say that? I am more comfortable in this room with you than anywhere else in the world. I don't think entertaining is as important as being safe or caring." She tensed after her admission. Her tongue, usually so disciplined, had a mind of its own today.

He sat up and leaned forward over his knees, bringing his person ever closer to hers, his eyes glinting from the dancing fire. "I have never received a greater compliment. Surely, it's the library and not me that entices you to this room."

"Perhaps," she lied, knowing that if she did not change the subject, that she might confess her heart. "Books are rather magical. I would wager my greatest talent is to glean hidden gems from even the most boring text."

He stared at her, as if he could see right through her useless attempt to throw boundaries around their conversation. Right when the mood between them sizzled as hot as the fire behind the grate, he sat back in his seat dousing it with needed air between them.

"You spoke of wagers and texts. I declare you prove your ability to me."

Elena sputtered. "Prove?"

"Shall we play a little game? We both select a few books and have a quarter of an hour to find something diverting, something inspiring, and something dreadfully boring in which to share with the other person."

"How will we determine the winner?" Elena asked.

"I think we are adult enough to vote between ourselves."

She loved the idea of spending more time with Anton, and it seemed that he wanted to spend more time with her as well. "And what is at stake if I should lose? Or is there an enticement to win?"

"Hmm . . . I overheard cook speaking with my mother this morning. She is making soup for dinner. The loser must slurp their soup very loudly."

"I couldn't." Elena laughed. "I fear you are used to making wagers with your brother and Mr. Gunther. What about a token? The winner must give up something precious to them."

"Like a dark secret?" his brow rose to an exaggerated height.

"Or a special button?" She lifted her own brows equally high.

"I could never take your prized buttons," Anton shook his head. "How about a swift kick to someone vexing? Or a kiss to someone undeserving? Yes, I think that's a valid consequence. The loser must give up a kiss to someone, and the winner chooses who that someone will be."

She scoffed. "This is your brilliant idea? I fear it is worse than the soup. I could be kissing a pig this time tomorrow."

"Or Mr. Gunther's grandfather . . ."

"Stop!" Elena giggled. "Your mischievousness is very un-earl-like."

"I have never been fond of gambling, but I do think the higher the stakes in this case, the better."

"And why is that?"

"Because I have never seen you this happy before. I believe this game is very important to your health."

"Because kissing a married gentleman twice my age is exactly what a doctor prescribes?"

"Well, yes." He pulled out his timepiece clipped to his vest pocket. "Oh, look, the game begins . . . now."

Elena squealed and jumped from her seat. She nearly tripped over the little tuffet as she raced to the shelf.

Anton laughed behind her but was equally enthusiastic in his stride to the other end of the shelf. He grabbed books left and right. He opened them and shut them again, before stacking them next to him on the floor. The pile grew higher and higher before Elena had managed to find the one book she thought would be the best for an entertaining text.

"I am worried about your methods." Anton's voice was nearly breathless.

Elena laughed. "At least I have a method. You are making a mess of the library."

"It will be worth it if I can find some needy gentleman who sorely lacks the confidence with the ladies. One generous kiss from you, and he will be skipping his way to matrimony."

Elena groaned as she shoved another unhelpful book back into place. "Since I will be the winner, I shall find you a sweet girl who has been pining for you since childhood. You will be her white knight."

"Clearly, you are not acquainted with the neighborhood."

"Didn't you hear about the picnic your sister and mother are planning? A few well-placed inquiries with Mary ought to do the trick."

"Thunder and turf!" Anton growled. He pulled books off the shelf at a greater pace, causing several to tumble to the floor. Interesting. There was at least one girl he was bent on avoiding.

Elena smothered her smile and selected her second book. She only needed something inspiring now. She turned and caught sight of the family Bible, turned on the shelf so its whole cover was facing forward. It was placed on the other side of a book end, giving it a place of distinction. She gasped. It was perfect! It was also on the other side of Anton. She moved behind him, but he deduced what she was moving toward.

"Blast!" he cried.

Strong arms encircled her waist and lifted her out of the way. For a moment, she forgot about their competition—her thoughts consumed by the sensation of being held. Anton released her abruptly and lunged for the Bible. Unfortunately, the stool was in the way and tripped him. Elena blinked away her stupor and sidestepped him. She managed to secure the Bible before he could get up.

Anton laughed from the floor. "You win this round."

"I intend to win them all," Elena said, darting to her seat with her three specially chosen books.

Anton groaned and hurried to finish selecting his items. "Just six minutes left."

"You're joking!" Elena thumbed through the Bible first, searching for the right verse to share. Her heart raced from the thrill of the competition. Anton took his seat with an armful, and Elena shook her head. There was no doubt now that she would win. She had the advantage of an extra minute and less books to search through.

The last minutes ticked by, and Anton finally called the time.

"All right. Should we start with boring?"

Elena put her hands to her temple. "This was much harder than I thought it would be. I needed a good half hour."

"Ha! I needed a good three days."

She held up her first book as if it were a great trophy. "For my boring text, I selected the dictionary. I have never met an individual who has ever read it all the way through."

"Very good," Anton said, impressed. He held up his book. "But I think many would find a dictionary interesting should they have the need for a word. My text contains the words boring, tedious, and dreary all on the same page. There is absolutely no room for argument here."

Elena shook her head. "Very well, I concede you outdid me. Shall we move to diverting passages? I found one from *Gulliver's Travels*. "*... a wife should be always a reasonable and agreeable companion, because she cannot always be young.*"

Anton chuckled. "A good one to be sure. Here is mine, a line from Shakespeare's *The Tempest*: *He receives comfort like cold oatmeal.*"

A laugh bubbled out of Elena. "Is that truly what the line says?"

"It is just here, come see."

Elena stood and moved to look over his shoulder. "So it is." Anton's head turned, and their vision connected. His lips curled into a sultry smile, and her eyes dropped to his mouth.

"So who is the winner of this round?" His soft words broke the strange connection between them, and Elena lurched back with surprise.

"Mine is written with greater wit, but yours is unexpected humor, which I can always appreciate."

"Do we call a tie?" Anton asked.

"Let us see who has found the most inspiring passage. I admit, I did not have time to choose a favorite verse. However, I have the most inspiring book, do I not? I shall open and read the first verse, and we shall see how it compares to yours." She opened the Bible. "Ah, Psalms. Excellent. *Forsake her not, and she shall preserve thee: love her . . .*"—Elena hesitated—"*. . . and she shall keep thee.*" Her cheeks warmed. "I, uh, imagined something of a different nature."

Anton's chuckle was low and rich, his gaze soft. "The Bible is full of revelatory passages." After an extended beat, he pulled a volume onto his lap. "Mine is from *An Essay Concerning Human Understanding* by John Locke. A favorite line says, *what worries you, masters you.*"

Elena repeated the words in her mind. What worries you, masters you. The truth rang inside of her louder than the clang of bells. She had been a slave to her worries for so long. Images of Bianca taunted her, and she squeezed her eyes shut. Paralyzing words pummeled her mind. *You are worthless. The fewer words you say, the less I pity the listener. You were not meant to wear color, since it would be better to blend in with the furniture than for anyone to have to look at you.* Years' worth of criticism flooded through her mind, and her head throbbed with the weight of it.

"Miss Muffet?"

Elena snapped her eyes open. "Yes?"

"You were a thousand miles away just now."

She gave a sheepish smile, trying to bury the pain her thoughts had resurrected. "Locke knew what he was saying, didn't he?"

"It's more a warning than an all-inclusive statement. I should like to think that worrying can motivate change and progression. It's when it consumes and paralyzes us that we know we are in trouble."

She swallowed. "Have you ever experienced such a state?"

"Me? Yes. I believe so. When my father died. I remember reading this then, and I promised myself I would not let my fears from my new position hold me back."

"Your courage is most impressive."

"I hardly think so. I've had my family's help. When we cannot progress alone, we must look to someone else who can carry us for a time. I discovered these words at the exact moment I needed them, and they could not be counted as coincidence. Divine arms always carry me the longest."

"I believe you have won, Lord Crawford. I shall forever remember these words. I have great need of them."

They were both quiet for a moment, before Anton broke the silence. "Let's forget the wager, shall we? I could never ask you to do anything that would make you uncomfortable." Anton's brow creased in the middle. "Should you ever need anything, Miss Muffet, I am your friend."

The words settled around her heart like a blanket, thawing the ice the flood of memories had caused. "I thank you." She was suddenly embarrassed under his watchful eye. "Mary and Sophia are likely wondering what is taking me so long."

"Go ahead, I can clean up in here."

"Are you sure?" She picked up the Bible and hurriedly returned it to its place.

"Please, go on. I will make a quick work of this."

"Very well." She tucked her shawl around her shoulders and pulled it close in front, stalling at the door. "Thank you." Those two simple words could never encapsulate her gratitude for their morning together, but it was all she had to give him.

She slipped out of the room and sighed. Would she ever meet a man equal to Anton after Bianca married? She would forever be ruined in love, having known what companionship and affection could be like and never having the opportunity to own it for herself.

Chapter 10

SEVERAL DAYS PASSED WITHOUT Elena meeting Anton at all. He had left to visit an old friend and was supposed to have returned yesterday. Her time at Banbury waned, and she was anxious to spend the duration of her visit with him. In his absence, had he thought of her at all?

She pulled out the thin sketchbook Mary had given her and sat in the drawing room to practice. A moment later, she registered voices just beyond the open door.

"You have returned." The sweet voice belonged to Sophia. The word return caught Elena's full attention.

"Just now. Yes." Anton's words were short and stilted.

"Did you enjoy your visit?"

"Yes."

Silence.

"Very good. I am glad to see you had a safe journey."

"Good day to you."

Elena frowned. While Elena's affection for Anton grew with each day, she did not know if he returned her feelings in any way. It hurt, even though she knew it was irrational. She was almost glad he did not come in and see her. She needed time to prepare a disinterested reaction to seeing him again.

Mary and Sophia found her a few moments later, and tea was called for. More wedding talk passed before Miss Bliss changed the conversation.

"Mary, what was Terrance like as a child?" Miss Bliss asked.

Mary clasped the handle of her teacup but did not raise it to her lips. "He knew what he wanted and he held to his course—very much like he is now. Oh, he did his best to impress Anton and Blake, and his wild ideas generally won them over."

"Their loyalty to each other is quite impressive," Miss Bliss said, reaching over and picking up a tart.

Mary grew thoughtful. "I was lucky if I could convince any of them to let me tag along. I preferred dolls to much of their play, but once in a while, I was set on convincing them I was just as good as any other boy."

"What about Lord Crawford?" Elena asked, as casually as she could. She hoped her cheeks did not betray her feelings. "Was he like his brother?"

Mary nodded. "All three of those boys were competitive and daring. Anton, though, was a deep thinker and often required alone time in the library where he was either lost in a book or in his own head."

Miss Bliss wiped the crumbs from her lap. "They all seem to have a protective nature about them too."

Mary groaned. "You should have seen how they were when Blake decided to court me. I still fear I will have to spend my married life with a brother on either side of me and Blake across the room."

They all laughed.

Mary turned to Elena. "What were you like as a child?"

"Oh, uh, I was quiet. Not much has changed there. I was like Lord Crawford and needed to be away from the others."

Mary likely didn't understand, but she smiled at Elena like she cared. "I can just imagine those large, blue eyes on a petite little child. I bet you were an absolute dream. You know, I wager blue is your color. Do you own any blue gowns?"

"No, my sister always said browns and grays suited me best." Though, her sister's intentions were for her to blend in, not stand out.

"Will you humor me and try on a few of my gowns? I have a lovely green one that is too small for me, and I just know it would fit you better."

Elena's eyes darted to Miss Bliss, who held no judgement in her eyes, then back to Mary. "If it would please you."

Mary shook her head. "Only if it pleases *you*."

To be given the choice was a true test of friendship. Elena nodded, quickly. "You have exquisite taste. I would feel honored if you think you could improve me."

"Not improve," Mary said, "just compliment."

A half hour later, Mary had a frown on her face, and Elena knew she had disappointed her new friend.

"None of these will do. You are far more petite than I realized." Mary sighed and sat on the edge of her bed.

"I wish I were not so tall," Sophia sighed.

"Nonsense," Mary said. "Terrance needed a tall woman to match him. Think how much less distance there is between you when you kiss."

Sophia giggled. "Terrance warned me about your boldness, but I agree. I think Terrance and I fit each other perfectly."

Mary grinned, but her smile fell as she turned to look at Elena. "I'm so sorry. It would have been a great deal more exciting to have a new dress to borrow for dinner."

Elena shrugged. "I don't mind. I only wished to please you."

"Well, of all the silliness. I only wished to please *you*!" Mary came over and linked arms with her. "I know you were planning on leaving before the wedding, but perhaps you could stay a few nights longer."

"Oh, yes," Sophia added. "It is such a small party. I don't know many of Terrance's friends, and I should like to have some of my own there."

"Me?" Elena whispered, disbelief stealing over her.

"Of course," Sophia said. "And I think we ought to have a dress for you commissioned for the occasion."

"It isn't as if I am the bride," Elena said, shaking her head.

Mary and Sophia looked at each other conspiratorially. "Not yet, anyway," Mary said.

Elena wished for a glimpse of their thoughts. "My mother did send some pin money with me. A new gown sounds terribly exciting." She couldn't hold back her grin.

Sophia rubbed her hands together. "We haven't long to get one made. We had better find a dressmaker right away."

Mary squeezed Elena's arm. "I was looking forward to the wedding before, but now I might just be looking forward to Elena's dress."

Sophia snorted and Elena had to cover her mouth to suppress her giggles. Banbury Castle might just be her favorite place in the world. What would Anton think if he saw her in a beautiful new gown? Would it even matter? She glanced at Sophia, with her golden curls and perfect complexion, and her smile drooped. How could Anton ever love Elena when Sophia, the most perfect person, still had his heart?

She forced her smile to return. Nothing need diminish the joy of a new dress.

Chapter 11

Anton wandered the corridors of his house hoping, but almost dreading, to run into Miss Muffet. He thought a quick trip to see a friend at their request would have cleared his mind. But he had never been so confused over a course of action in his life. When he thought of something amusing, he wondered if she would think the same. He even wanted her opinion about the concerns he had for his friend.

Miss Muffet was not who he ever thought he would fall in love with. He remembered her odd mannerisms at the house party— the way she would turn away from every conversation, hide in a book, and avoid anything living. Surely, such behavior was abnormal. His recent time with her contradicted all those previous thoughts. The odd, petite woman had become attractive to him. He needed to see her again to understand exactly how he felt about her.

He turned the corner and froze. It was as if his wish had brought her presence. There she was, standing a few feet from him in the corridor, wearing one of her drab, brown dresses, her head bent over a letter.

The ivory, crocheted collar added a spinster look to a person so young. She had not seen him yet, and his pulse thrummed as he studied her profile. Gone were the curls in front. She had pulled all of her hair back from her face, accentuating her creamy skin and neck. Instead of the tight little bun, soft curls now piled at the crown.

He took a cautious step toward her, his heart finally agreeing with his head. He didn't care what the world thought—this was the woman for him. She had changed in so many ways and had blossomed into someone he knew he wanted to spend the rest of his life getting to know better. His shoes were damp from walking the grounds with Patches and squeaked with his footfall.

Her head whipped toward him, exposing a tear-streaked cheek.

"Miss Muffet?" His hesitant step took purpose, and he strode toward her. "What is the matter?

"Nothing." She clenched the letter to her chest.

Why was her guard back up? Was it because he had been gone? "Have you received bad news?"

"No. It is from my home. Why should such news disturb me?"

"You must be homesick then."

"Yes, that is it. I miss my home. It won't be long now, and I can return. Excuse me." She pushed past him and hurried away.

He stared at her, his mind racing. What had just happened? He had been anxious to greet her, but she did not seem to return such thoughts. He reached up and rubbed the back of his neck under his cravat. Didn't she trust him yet? Maybe this was not meant to work between them. He couldn't force her to bring him into her confidence, nor to care for him.

An hour before dinner, Sophia's parents and grandmother arrived. Lord Neeley was similar in age to what Anton's father would be, if he were still alive, and Lady Neeley held her youth much like his own mother—with hardly a gray hair between them.

"Welcome," Mother said to their guests. "We have been so eager to have you come. Sophia just went to change for dinner, but I shall send a maid to tell her you have arrived."

A footman held Sophia's grandmother's arm, a woman unstable even with her cane.

"Thank you," Lord Neeley said, putting his arm around Sophia's grandmother. "This is my mother, Lady Margaret Neeley. She prefers everyone to call her Marg, as she is hard of hearing and often gets lost in such a long title."

"We are pleased to have you, Marg," Anton said in a loud voice before bowing.

"Is this Mr. Hastings?" Marg asked, her voice as wobbly as she was.

"No, dear," Lady Neeley leaned near Marg's ear. "This is his brother."

"The earl?"

"Yes, Lord Crawford."

Marg nodded and pushed up her spectacles. They reminded Anton of the ones Miss Muffet used to wear.

"He's not married?" Marg asked, turning so Anton could answer.

"No, your ladyship," he said. This summer he had begun to resent being single, and his wandering thoughts about Miss Muffet seemed to add to his growing discontentment.

The guests were shown to their room where they could change for dinner, and Anton found himself wandering to his own room.

At dinner, Anton was seated farther from Miss Muffet because of the guests. He stole a glance in her direction, but her head was bent low over her meal, much like when she had first arrived.

"How long have you been here, Miss Muffet?" Lady Neeley asked. "I am happy to see you again."

"Nearly a month," Miss Muffet answered, her voice subdued.

"How wonderful. I had no idea."

"I have invited her to stay for the wedding, Mama." Sophia smiled at Miss Muffet. Miss Muffet's sudden smile confused Anton. He thought she was ready to return home. "She has written to her parents, and we are hoping they will permit her to stay longer."

"These three girls have become quite inseparable," Mother explained to Lady Neeley.

Gunther groaned. "I fear after we wed, Mary will regret she cannot keep planning her wedding with her friends." Several amused chuckles reverberated around the table.

Lord Neeley reached for his goblet. "What is this I hear about a picnic?"

"Papa, you must come." Sophia turned in her seat to touch her father's arm. "It will be a chance to meet a few members of the neighborhood."

"Looks like I will have to turn in early tonight so I don't sleep through it."

Anton glanced down at Miss Muffet again. This time she was looking at him. Was she hoping he would help her get out of staying longer at Banbury? Did she need his help talking to his overbearing sister? Mary could be quite the storm, should she choose to be.

When dinner ended, the men stayed for port until Lord Neeley declared his intentions to retire for the night. "I don't travel well in a carriage. My mother wouldn't hear of me riding alongside. She can't see well out the window, and she worries so."

"Of course," Anton said. "You must see to your health." They all murmured goodnight, and he and the men moved into the drawing room where the ladies were visiting.

Everyone naturally paired off. Terrance sat by Sophia, Gunther by Mary, Mother by Lady Neeley, and Anton was drawn to Miss Muffet. Four people did not fit comfortably on the sofa, so when Mary and Gunther sat on the other end of them, Miss Muffet was forced to squish closer to Anton. Her small thigh pressed close to his. Their hands brushed, and she quickly moved hers to her lap.

What was clearly uncomfortable to her was anything but for him. "Are you feeling better than when I last saw you?"

"Yes, I am well." Her words did not match her sober expression.

"Did I miss anything of importance while I was away?" he asked.

"No, I should think not. We met with a dressmaker, and Terrance interviewed a possible cook for his estate."

"And what were the outcomes?"

Miss Muffet looked over to Mary and Gunther conversing next to them, then finally turned her face to him. "From what I hear, everything turned out as expected."

Why was she being so tight-lipped? He hesitated, knowing the question he asked was more for her benefit than his own. "Would you like me to tell the others that you are ready to return home? They will understand."

"No!" Her vehement response surprised him.

"Oh." Perhaps he had misread her. "My apologies. I did not mean to overstep."

She shook her head, clearly flustered. "How did you find your friend?"

He chose not to press her and answered her question. "He is prone to melancholy and was deeply depressed in spirit. He usually fairs better in the summer, but I knew as soon as I received his letter, he needed me. We met at school, and he latched on to me—though he hated Gunther."

Miss Muffet gave him a hint of a smile. "He likes someone a little more serious."

"Yes, but I can never be too serious when I am with him. He feeds off of negative energy."

"Are your visits draining?"

Anton sighed. "You might say so."

"You are a good friend to go to him when he needs you."

She always had a way of making him feel like he was the most chivalrous person in the world. "Who do you turn to when you need someone?"

Her brows raised. "Me? I . . . I write in my diary."

"Really? I do the same. And when you are done? Do you feel better?"

"Mostly. I usually eat something sweet if writing did not help."

Anton shook his head. "I can just see you pilfering the contents of the larder while everyone is asleep."

"I would never do it while anyone was awake."

Her serious expression made him laugh.

"What's so amusing?" Mary asked, turning her body away from Gunther to face them.

"She hates to miss a good joke," Gunther explained.

Anton shook his head. "I would never reveal Miss Muffet's secret midnight snacks." He looked at her, wondering if she would take offense to his public tease. When she chuckled, he relaxed. If they were to marry, she would have to be able to take a little teasing if they were to survive his family.

Marry? His smile slipped. Was he thinking so seriously about her? It made sense that if he cared for her, marriage would be the next plausible step.

"I am sorry if I am better at stealing food than any of you." Miss Muffet's quip made his smile return. Finally, she was relaxed again in his presence. Maybe he should not have left her alone for three days. She needed an ally with all these engaged couples. But would she stay long enough to give him a chance to sort through his feelings and make a decision about the future?

Chapter 12

The overcast sky did not stop the picnic preparations, nor did Elena let a disheartening letter keep her from participating. Blankets were draped like a patchwork across the courtyard and around the few trees. Servants set up a table for the food, carrying tray after tray with delicious items. Families began arriving in the late afternoon with a handful of children shepherded by their nursemaids. Anton had been busy greeting guests and seeing to arrangements, so Elena kept close to Mary and Mr. Gunther. There was something about Banbury and the Crawford family that breathed new strength into her, giving her permission to enjoy life while she could.

"I am eager for you to meet Blake's parents." Mary tucked her legs underneath her and smoothed her dress. "Be warned. My future mother-in-law can be quite intimidating. Oh look! There is Lord Templeton."

Gunther, who was leaning against a tree with his legs spread out, choked on his drink and coughed into his arm.

Mary put her hand on Gunther's back. "I did not mean anything by it. I thought only to introduce him to Elena."

Gunther wiped his face with a napkin. "Can Terrance do the favor? I hardly think it appropriate for *you* to make the introduction."

Mary turned a beaming face to Elena. "Isn't he darling when he is jealous? I do believe Lord Templeton is coming this way. Blake Gunther, be on your best behavior."

A fine-dressed gentleman with dark hair and pleasing features weaved around the clusters of people, intent in their direction.

"Who is he?" Elena asked.

Mr. Gunther answered for Mary. "He is new to the neighborhood, and I have already made an enemy of him."

"Have you?" Elena asked. She could not imagine anyone truly disliking the amiable man next to her, even if he was a bit of a dandy.

"He had eyes for Mary, and I am clearly the better man for her." Mr. Gunther said, his voice dropping to a whisper as Lord Templeton stepped up to their blanket.

"Mr. Gunther," Lord Templeton tipped his hat. "Lady Mary." He looked at Elena. "I do not believe we've met."

"This is my favorite friend, Miss Muffet," Mary said. "Miss Muffet, meet Lord Templeton."

Elena would never tire of hearing Mary's affectionate words.

Lord Templeton bowed. "It is a pleasure to make your acquaintance. Are you visiting the castle then?"

"Yes." Meeting a stranger was easier than in the past, but she still had to remind herself to look him in the eyes. "I hope to stay for the wedding." Her gaze sought out Terrance and Sophia, only a few feet away, speaking with the rector.

"Of course," Lord Templeton followed her line of vision. "I was hoping to gain an introduction to Mr. Hasting's intended today. I have heard a great deal about her from the family."

"Then you are here often?" Miss Muffet asked. It seemed strange that he knew much of Miss Bliss when Elena had never heard or seen this man, and she had been there for several weeks. The engagement of Mary to Mr. Gunther was surely the reason. This poor man was one of many thwarted in matrimonial pursuits. She felt instant sympathy for him.

"Lady Crawford has been exceptionally generous to me. I have had the pleasure of becoming friends with both Mr. Hastings and Lord Crawford, though I have lived here not two months."

At the mention of Lord Crawford's name, Elena did her best to resist seeking him out with her gaze and focused on Lord Templeton. "We are both fortunate in our friendship."

Lord Templeton's eyes were soft and kind. She liked him immediately, and she wondered if it was because of his friendship with Anton that made her able to trust him so quickly.

"Everyone in this neighborhood is most exceptional. I am drawn to the history here too. This castle alone tells many stories. Have you seen the foundation stone?"

"No, I have not had the pleasure."

Mary put her hand on Elena's arm. "Oh, but you must. It's a favorite tale of my family."

"Allow me to show you," Lord Templeton said. "I remember such few names of people here. I would be glad for an excuse to walk with you."

"Is it far?" Elena did not want to miss speaking with Anton when he finished his duty as host.

"It is just around the back of the keep."

"Very well." Elena climbed to her feet and walked alongside Lord Templeton. They passed the refreshment table and walked away from the others.

"The stone has two stories to it," Lord Templeton began. "There are those who believe it is a faerie stone which blesses or curses the inhabitants of the castle based on their good works."

"And what is the second story?"

"That it is just an ordinary rock."

Elena giggled. She would choose to believe the first story, since Banbury castle allowed her to laugh whenever she chose to.

There was a swish of legs walking behind them, and she turned to find Anton coming toward them.

"Crawford," Lord Templeton said in greeting. "I thought there would be rain today and the picnic would be canceled."

Anton blew out his breath. "Yes, my mother has been worried about nothing else since yesterday. She thrives when hosting, and yet, it wears me out just to watch her." Anton's gaze swung to meet Elena's. "Are you enjoying yourself, Miss Muffet?"

"Indeed. Lord Templeton was about to show me the castle's foundation stone." Did he approve? Something about his stance looked wary, but of what, Elena was not sure.

Anton looked from her to Lord Templeton. "Might I join you?"

"Won't your guests miss you?" Lord Templeton asked.

"I think they can spare me for a few minutes. They all came to see Miss Bliss anyway."

Elena wondered if Lord Templeton knew about Anton's feelings for Miss Bliss. And what would they both think if they knew Elena's feelings for Anton?

"Shall we?" Anton urged them all forward.

Elena fell into step between the two men.

"Miss Muffet—" Both men started at the same time.

Anton motioned for Lord Templeton to speak first.

"Where are you visiting from?"

"Heythrop," she replied.

"Oh, that isn't too far from here."

"No, but I regret this is my first time to Banbury."

Lord Templeton put his hands behind his back. "It is a hidden treasure, is it not?"

"Yes." Miss Muffet stole a glance at Anton. He studied the ground as they walked. Perhaps he had forgotten what he wanted to say. The need to include him in the conversation felt necessary, but she was still honing her newfound social skills. "Lord Crawford, is there any other tidbits of history about Banbury that I have not been made aware of?"

He lifted his gaze to hers. "More than I could tell you in this short walk. These old stones have seen both bloodshed and glory." He stopped at the corner of the keep and pointed to the bottom. "That blackish stone there is the one Lord Templeton was referring to. It's not much to look at, but more eyes have studied it than any other in this great edifice."

Elena stepped forward and caught her foot on a loose rock. She stumbled, and soon both men had a hold of each of her arms.

"Forgive my clumsiness," she said, heat filling her cheeks. Lord Templeton seemed reluctant to release her, but he did. Anton, however, did not. Two very handsome, and extremely worthy, gentlemen were both giving her all of their attention. What had she done to deserve it?

"Care to make a wish before we return to the others?" Anton asked.

"Does this stone grant wishes too?"

"Just one."

She bent her head back to look into his eyes. "Did you use yours up as a child?"

"I've been saving it."

"All these years?"

"I didn't want to waste it. Gunther wished for a horse, and he got one. Terrance wished for a new sled, and he got one. It might just be an ugly rock, but it's held quite a bit of magic for us."

Lord Templeton chuckled, and she remembered he was still standing right next to them. "No one told me about this wish business."

Anton gave an exaggerated frown. "We try to be discreet in case the enchantment runs out. I trust you understand."

Lord Templeton bowed. "I swear to never reveal the full power of the Banbury stone."

With a quick nod, Anton released Elena. "Very well, you may both touch the stone and speak your wish."

"Aloud?" Elena asked. She wanted to make a wish but could never do so with these men watching.

"In your mind is sufficient."

She wondered if he had said that merely to put her at ease. She stepped forward just the same, bent over, and touched the stone. In her mind, she wished with all her heart to have Anton's love. Lord Templeton put his hand down next to hers, and her concentration broke. Pulling back, she almost laughed at herself. The likelihood of her getting her wish was nigh impossible.

Anton cleared his throat. "I should get back to my guests."

"I will join you," she added quickly. She turned to see what Lord Templeton would say, but he was still staring at the stone.

"Go ahead," Lord Templeton said. "I will follow in a moment."

Anton put out his arm, and Elena accepted it. He motioned back with his head when they were out of earshot. "He is taking his wish very seriously."

"I could say as much about you."

He grinned. "Yes, you are right. But I think I finally know what I want." His eyes met hers, and they seemed brighter than normal.

Why did she feel breathless beneath his gaze? "Is this a private wish like mine?"

"For now." His hand came up and rested on top of hers, making her arms erupt in gooseflesh.

If only she could suspend time, then this moment would last forever. Tomorrow—and the end of her happiness—would never come.

Chapter 13

Rain pelted against Anton's bedroom window as he dressed for the day. The weather had held long enough for them to enjoy their picnic the day before, but it had poured heavily all night long. Thoughts of the picnic made him think of his earlier frustration with Lord Templeton. His friend had found Elena to be an attractive, amiable young lady, and it bothered Anton a great deal.

Despite these feelings, he found his jealousy easier to conquer with Lord Templeton than he had with his brother. It had taken seeing Sophia again to realize she did not own his heart but had deeply wounded his pride. Lord Templeton's attention toward Miss Muffet had accomplished something else entirely. It had helped Anton be sure of his plans for the future. He did want Elena in his life. He was infinitely happy to have her on his arm and sad and anxious when she stepped away. He had overcomplicated the idea of love and almost missed it when it was right in front of him. He had Lord Templeton to thank for that, so he couldn't very well be angry with him.

Now he just needed to tell Elena. He bent over washstand in his room, adjusting the cravat his valet had tied for him. He took a deep breath and examined himself in the mirror. Looking presentable was one thing, but being collected inside was different. Having never done this, he wasn't sure where to start. He practiced his speech in the mirror half a dozen times before he felt ready to face her.

He made his way down for breakfast, realizing he was much later than usual. He possessed more cowardice than he realized. Shaking his hands at his side to loosen his nerves, he stepped into the dining room. However, the image before him made him stop abruptly.

"I see you are as surprised as the rest of us," Mother said, her posture anything but relaxed. She came and stood beside him. "You remember Mr. and Mrs. Muffet and their oldest daughter."

Instead of focusing on Mr. Muffet's stern expression or the way Elena's sister batted her eyelashes in his direction, Anton's eyes found Elena. His mouth went dry when he saw her at the end of the table, spectacles back on, her head bowed, and her gaze refusing to meet his.

He forced his attention back to his guests and bowed to the family. They passed the usual cordial greetings and sat back down to breakfast, along with Sophia and her parents, Terrance, and Mary. Their long oak table was quite crowded.

He was still processing what this would mean to his courting plans while he filled his plate at the sideboard with his breakfast. The sound of the conversation nearest him floated over to his ears.

"Do you have to leave right away?" Mother asked Mr. Muffet. "This storm is dreadful! You are welcome to break your journey here for a day or two."

Mr. Muffet shook his head. "Bianca insisted on bringing her sister back home. I am afraid we weren't prepared for such unfavorable weather."

Mother seemed as disappointed as he was. "We wrote requesting to keep Elena longer. We are so sorry to see her go. Please, consider at least a night here so we might have a proper farewell."

Anton turned in time to see Mr. Muffet look at his wife, who seemed to beg with her eyes for the same thing. Anton wondered if Mr. Muffet had the heart to listen to his wife. He had spent some time with the couple at Sophia's house party and had not taken Mr. Muffet to be a very generous man.

Mr. Muffet seemed more annoyed than thrilled with the idea of staying. "Surely one night will allow the ground to soak up some of the torrents of water on the road. Do you have room for us? We were just discussing staying at the inn in town."

"Yes, of course," Anton said, joining the conversation.

Mother grinned. "Wonderful! I shall inform my staff as soon as you have eaten, and they shall prepare your rooms."

Anton exhaled with relief and set his plate down in an empty seat next to his mother. He glanced down the table to see Mary trying to speak to Elena. Elena did not respond, and Mary's countenance showed her frustration and disappointment. Anton's chest tightened with apprehension. What was bothering her? This was the old Elena, not the one he had come to know. And blast the timing of all of this. He had just decided to tell Elena his feelings, and now she was going home.

When breakfast ended, Anton hoped to catch Elena, but her sister snagged her and carted her off. Anton couldn't bear to make small talk with anyone, so he made his way to the library. Something very wrong was happening in his home and with Elena, but he couldn't grasp what it was.

Elena reluctantly led the way to her bedroom under Bianca's orders. When they reached the room, Bianca nudged her inside with a sharp poke of her elbow. The door swung shut behind them, and Elena faced her sister. A person wasn't supposed to wake up to find themselves in a bad dream. What she wouldn't give to crawl back into her bed and go back to yesterday when her arm was tucked safely in Anton's. Surely, she would never get such an opportunity again—not if Bianca had her way.

"How dare you come here!" Bianca growled through gritted teeth.

"M—Mother planned it all."

"So she says, but you must have given her the idea. All those books have fed your imagination. You schemed up this grand escape, didn't you?" Bianca set her hands on her hips, scowling fiercely at her.

"I promise, I did no such thing." Elena backed away a step. What would Bianca do to punish her? Her sister was never predictable, except that Elena would pay in some way.

Bianca sneered. "It doesn't matter. We will be leaving, and you will regret ever coming here."

Elena bowed her head and retreated another step. Agreeing with her sister was the best course of action. She knew from past experiences that arguing only incited her.

"I'm going downstairs, but you are to stay here. You have a headache and won't be able to even eat dinner tonight. If you happen to see anyone before we leave, you will not speak to them. If they press you, say something to make them forget you forever."

The reality of her change in circumstances pressed against Elena's chest and threatened to suffocate her. Obeying Bianca in the past had been a way to keep some semblance of peace. Now, it seemed like she was being asked to summit a mountain of slippery glass. How could she turn against her new friends? It would be better to feign an illness than to "make them forget her," as Bianca had said.

Bianca did not wait for Elena to agree—she was used to Elena doing exactly as she commanded. Her sister departed, and the door thudded behind her. Without an ounce of hope, Elena's knees quaked. Soon she was on the floor, her face in her hands. Her spirit groaned within her, but she could not utter a sound. She could barely breathe. Was there no way to escape her sister? She had one last night at Banbury Castle, but she was paralyzed with despair and could think of no possible plan to save herself.

Chapter 14

Anton made the circuit through the corridors and back to the library several times throughout the day but to no avail. Elena kept to her room. It would not be proper to try to seek her there, but he could not exactly coax her out either. He needed a middleman. He needed Mary.

He found Mary sketching a picture in her bedroom. "What are you doing here? It isn't like you to miss a chance to visit with company."

Mary put her sketchbook aside. "Blake hasn't come to see me today."

"It's pouring rain," Anton said. "Will you begrudge him for caring for his health?"

"No," she sighed. "But Elena is acting strange, and I am very put off with her family for ruining our plans. I need Blake to make me feel better."

"He does all that for you?"

"Yes. He listens and holds my hand. Can't he sense that I need him?"

Anton wondered if he could sense Elena's needs. Right now, he could only think of his own. He had a powerful need to speak with Elena.

"I need your help with something important."

"Please don't ask me to entertain Bianca. Sophia already warned me about her, and I am not in the mood to be pleasant."

Anton folded his arms across his chest. "I heard from Terrance that Miss Bianca Muffet did not care for Miss Bliss at the house party. Is that what you mean?"

Mary shrugged. "She just said Bianca could be very demanding and sulky if she did not get her way. I know how much you want us to help with yours and Mama's hosting responsibilities, but can't we just leave them to themselves?"

Anton shook his head. "It's about Elena."

"Elena?" Mary's eyebrows shot up. "Since when do you call her by her given name?"

Anton hadn't noticed his slip. "Never mind that. I need you to speak with her and arrange a way for the two of us to meet."

Mary's brows remained arched in surprise. "Anton, do you care for Elena?"

The question did not rattle him as he thought it would. "If you expect me to tell you the intimate workings of my heart before I tell Elena, you are wrong. Will you do it or not?"

Mary's lips curled upward. "I commend your choice, dear brother. She will be an excellent match for you."

Anton didn't have time for this. "Come, Mary. Will you help me? She won't leave her room, and time is ticking."

Jumping to her feet, Mary put her hands on either side of Anton's arms. "Leave it to me. And look, I am no longer melancholy!" She practically skipped out of the room. Anton squeezed his eyes shut and slumped onto the edge of her bed. He didn't know how long he would have to wait. A woman rarely did anything fast if it involved talking.

A soft knock sounded on her door before it opened a crack. Mary stuck her head through the opening.

"May I come in?"

Elena sat up in her bed. "I . . . I'm not feeling well."

"Oh, no. Should I have some headache powders sent up?"

Elena needed to get rid of Mary before Bianca found them together. There was no way she would let Bianca bring harm to any of her dear friends. "I'm well enough. I need rest is all."

"Anton hopes to meet you in the library. It's very important. Are you up for it?"

Elena shook her head quickly. "I . . . I couldn't."

Instead of looking sympathetic though, Mary smiled. "It won't take long, and then you can rest." Mary slipped inside the room and closed the door behind her. "You should wear your blue dress. I know we wanted to save it for the wedding, but since you are leaving, you should wear it now."

"But I'm sick."

Mary nodded. "I know, but you'll have plenty of time to recover. What he has to say will not take long." She pulled out the gown of choice and gushed over it anew. "This turned out so well."

Elena sputtered. "Really, Mary. This is too much. I'm not wearing the dress, and I don't want you in here. You need to leave." Mary froze, likely from the harsh sound of Elena's voice. Elena repeated, "You need to leave."

"I don't understand." Mary's confused expression pierced through Elena's resolve, and she almost relented. She only had to think of past experiences of Bianca's wrath to fortify herself once more.

"Please, Mary."

Mary set the dress down and reluctantly left. The moisture in Elena's throat stung as she resisted the tears. She hated herself. Elena fell back in her bed and begged for sleep to overcome her.

"Well?" Anton asked, when Mary returned.

Mary shook her head. If she was depressed before, now she was nearly despondent.

"What happened?" He climbed off the bed and moved to Mary's side.

"I don't know. She was sharp with me. I cannot understand it. What did I do to offend her?"

"I cannot imagine Elena acting that way." Maybe Anton didn't know her like he thought he did.

"Have I lost a good friend?" Mary asked.

Anton put his hand gently on her arm. "She is likely upset that she has to return home so soon. There are things about her even I don't know."

Mary lifted her eyes to meet his. "You are probably right, but I have failed you. She will not meet you."

Acute disappointment twisted his stomach in knots. He nodded and left the room. He had just told Mary not to take Elena's behavior personally, but now he was acting sensitive. His case was hopeless. That night, Elena did not come down for dinner. Anton barely slept, and he was up by dawn. The family was still abed the next morning when Anton found himself in the courtyard facing the Banbury Stone.

"You know why I am here, don't you?" He couldn't help talking to the rock. He'd done it since he was a child. "I finally made up my mind. It isn't to grow taller than my younger brother, or to resurrect my father, or a hundred other wishes in my heart. I think I know what would make me happy. I want a wife and children. I want to grow old in these walls and see my posterity thrive. I want . . . I want Miss Elena Muffet to be my bride."

He bent down and put his hand on the rock, and though the wish passed through his mind, he was no longer concentrating on the rock. He was communing with God, praying for a blessing that he could not give himself. She needed to return his love, and he needed to deserve it.

"Father in Heaven, thou knowest the desire of my heart. Help me."

"I wish you could stay for the wedding," Mary said at breakfast.

Elena wished for the same. She hated to say goodbye to Mary, but she had been grateful for one last moment without Bianca to smooth things over before they left.

"Please forgive me for yesterday. I was not myself."

Mary nodded. "Of course."

Bianca strode into the room and sat down opposite them. Elena swallowed and forced herself to say in a brusk tone, "I didn't really care to attend the wedding. I would much prefer to return home."

"Are you sure?" Mary blinked, hurt and confusion clouding her eyes.

"Yes, I am quite sure. There isn't a single reason for me to stay." The words felt like bile on her tongue, burning and hateful.

She caught movement at the door and saw Anton standing there. His face paled, and he looked as if he had been slapped. She hated herself so much in that moment that she couldn't remain seated. Jumping to her feet, she darted past Anton. She dashed down the corridors and up the stairs to her bedchamber. Throwing open the door, she froze in the threshold. There on her bed was her new blue gown with deep slashes through the fabric.

No!. A sharp pain pierced her chest, and she clutched her racing heart. No, no, no!

She felt someone come up behind her. She turned and saw the same stunned face on Sophia. Her friend was taller and could easily see the damage over Elena's head.

"Why would you do such a thing?" Mortification lanced across Sophia's beautiful face.

"I . . . I . . ." Her only friends thought the worst of her. Her lost joy was replaced with sheer agony. She pushed past Sophia and hurried back down the stairs. She barely registered Anton's and Mary's forms in the corridor as she flew past them. Before she knew it, she was outside in the rain and running past the garden toward the orchard.

"Elena! Elena, stop!"

She knew Anton's voice, but she would not stop even to hear him call her by her given name again. Her life was ruined. She had tasted happiness, and she could not ever return to her former life. She would keep running until she was far, far away. She had no plans, just to escape and start new somewhere else. The splotched spectacles blinded her, so she ripped them from her face and pushed herself to run faster.

The rain soaked her gown through, and it clung to her legs as she ran. Her feet slid a few times, but she righted herself and pushed on. She was sure she had lost Anton but did not dare look behind her. Past the meadow, she turned into a copse of trees, not knowing what was beyond them. Her panic launched anew when Patches began barking, the noise growing ever closer. She stopped for a moment and leaned against the rough bark of a tree to catch her breath. Patches caught up with her.

"Go away! Please, go away!"

"Elena!"

She turned and saw Anton drawing closer. Thunder rumbled in the sky, and she bolted again, but she was not fast enough. After a few strides, he caught her arm and pulled her to a stop. She bent her head and turned away from him. He put his other hand on her arm so he was holding both her shoulders.

"I saw your sister when you were speaking to Mary. I don't know what's happened, but I know you are acting the way you are because of her. I don't believe you want to leave here. Please, tell me I am right. Tell me the truth!"

Elena shook her head.

"Elena, I am not going to let you be anywhere near your sister until I know you are safe." His gaze caught hers.

"Why do you care? Why can't you leave me be?"

"Because . . . Because I love you."

Elena's agony tripled at his words. She wanted to be with him so much it hurt, but it also hurt to think of Bianca secretly destroying their lives in any way she could. Elena tried to pull away, but he tugged her closer. Her resistance crumbled, and she fell into his arms and sobbed.

"Darling," he whispered, against her wet hair. "I can't help you if you don't tell me."

"I cannot," she cried. She also couldn't leave the protection of his arms. She wanted to savor this moment to carry with her for the rest of her life.

"Don't let your worries control you, remember?"

She choked back a sob and nodded against him. "It's so hard."

"I will carry you. Please, let me carry you."

"It won't work. If she learns I care for you, she will make you regret ever looking at me. She will do it, I promise. She has tortured me my entire life."

Anton's arms tightened around her. "She cannot hurt me. I won't let anything happen."

Bianca was manipulative and unforgiving. What if she poisoned his food or spread rumors to hurt his career in parliament? She would not put either past her sister anymore. Her chest tightened with fear, and she pushed against his chest and stepped away from him. "Once my sister is married, my circumstances could change. Until then, I am not worthy of your attention."

"You are more than worthy." His eyes bore into hers. "My whole family sees what you cannot. I assure you, there is no need to wait until your sister marries." When she could not agree, he shook his head in frustration. "Elena, I don't want to wait for what could never happen."

Elena took another defeated step backward. "I could never ask you to."

"Please, let me speak with your father."

Elena shook her head, tears and rain blurring her vision. "It is enough to know you care."

He sighed. "It is not enough for me. I want a chance to fight for it."

She searched his eyes. "What if fighting causes more contention? I will be forced to endure more than I can bear."

"Do you trust me?"

Wiping rain from her cheeks, she nodded.

He stepped closer and tucked a wet lock of hair behind her ear. "As Eve says to Adam in *Paradise Lost*, 'thou to me art all things under heav'n.' We will do this together."

Peace and hope cradled her heart like none she had ever experienced. Her smile was slow but steady. "Your words give me courage."

He stared at her, and his somber lips finally pulled into a smile to match hers. "A kiss is more powerful than words." His warm hands gently brought her closer. The rain danced rivets on his face, but all she saw were his lips. They were cold as they met her mouth, but when his lips parted, warmth passed from him to her. His hand moved to the small of her back, and the space between them disappeared. His kiss deepened and, like a poem, became an expression of all their feelings. She lost herself in their embrace, in the movements of his mouth, and the feel of his arms protecting her from the frightening outside world.

She heard shouting before she truly registered that that someone was her father. She pulled away and saw him half-running toward them. Clutching Anton's jacket, she cowered. His hands stroked her back, calming her in a way she had never experienced. His touch diminished her panic almost as quickly as it had come.

"Lord Crawford, I hope you mean to ask for my daughter." Her father panted for air. "After what I've just seen, who knows what has happened during her stay here."

"I do," Anton shouted over the wind and rain. "I want to marry her straightaway."

The anger seemed to drain from her father's posture. "Oh. Very well, then. If you insist." A semblance of a smile crossed his face. Surely, he knew the connection to an earl would benefit his own position.

Anton wasn't finished though. "I should like to have her reside here until the wedding. Under my protection."

"Do you mean to insinuate that I cannot protect her myself?"

Anton found Elena's hand. "I believe this conversation would be better finished inside before your daughter catches cold."

Mr. Muffet agreed, and the three of them made their way back to the house.

Mary, Mrs. Muffet, and Bianca were waiting for them just inside the vestibule.

"I told you, Father," Bianca said. "She practically threw herself on him."

"She did no such thing," Anton corrected.

Elena put her hand up to silence him. He seemed surprised by that, as did her father. "Please, let me explain." She stepped away from Anton and faced her sister. "I have let you control me for too long, but never again. I'm not returning home with you, and you will be powerless to touch me again." She turned to her parents. "It was Bianca who insisted I claim the role of the younger daughter in public, not me. It was by her insistence that I wear the spectacles, the drab gowns, and never speak in public." As she said it, she realized not defending herself all these years did not bring her family peace—it solidified the discord.

"Don't listen to her!" Bianca screeched. "She is lying to you."

Elena beseeched Mary next. "I was made to feel guilty if I spoke to anyone and felt unworthy of friendship."

Bianca shook her head fervently. "They already feel sorry for you without you telling tales. Why would they want to be friends with someone like you?" She turned to Mary. "She is always doing things like this—pinching herself and blaming me."

Anton reached over and squeezed Elena's hand. Courage rose inside of her, lifting her from the bonds of fear that had paralyzed her for so long. "It is your word against mine, but I will no longer be wrapped in your web of lies. I am going to marry Lord Crawford."

"No!" Bianca said incredulously.

Elena could suddenly see her sister as she really was—an insecure girl, desperate for affection. "My being married first will not make you any less of a person, Bianca. My existence in this life isn't a disadvantage to you. You can still change as I have done. And as much as I have grown to despise you, I will not let hatred destroy my spirit. I am going to work every day to forgive you. You have no more power over me." As she said it, she felt her own albatross fall from her neck. Elena's heart was finally free.

Mr. Muffet cleared his throat. "The girls haven't fought like this for years."

"That's because you haven't *paid attention* for years," Mrs. Muffet said. "Bianca, you have always craved attention, and I fear it has not been in the best of ways. We have failed you both, and I promise to remedy it."

"Me?" Bianca shook her head. "It's all her! She's lying! You cannot prove any of this."

Elena pushed back a wet stand of hair from off her cheek. "Perhaps not, but I have kept a detailed log in my journal and am in possession of several threatening letters."

Bianca gasped. "One more word, and I will see you ruined. I'll cut off all your hair while you sleep, and no man will ever want you."

Her mother gasped. "Bianca!"

Mr. Muffet reached over and grabbed his daughter by the arm. "That's enough, young lady. We will speak of this at home. Elena, you will stay here until the wedding. Lord Crawford, please refrain from any more orchard romance until this is legal and done."

Anton put his arm around Elena. "Yes, sir."

Mr. Muffet pulled Bianca out of the room while she yelled all sorts of vile threats over her shoulder. Elena shivered and Anton pulled her closer.

"You were as brave as a regal lioness facing off an opportunistic jackal," Anton whispered into her hair. "You can breathe now. You're safe."

Mary went over to her other side. "Safe and loved—by all of us."

Elena swallowed back more tears. Words wouldn't come. All she could do was nod. Anton sensed her need to be held and tucked her close to him.

Chapter 15

A THOUSAND POETS COULD not put to words the love Anton felt for Elena. She stood illuminated in light by the window, wearing a beautiful light-green dress—one of Mary's taken in for her until more could be made. Her hair was pulled away from her face with just a few loose tendrils by her temples. And an added boon, Anton had caught her alone while the rest of the house prepared for Terrance and Sophia's wedding.

He did his best to quietly approach, but she heard him and turned. A smile lit her face, making her whole countenance blossom like a rose.

"Why are you looking at me that way?" she asked.

Anton reached her and caught her hands with his. "Did you not know a man always looks at the woman he loves this way?"

She raised a brow. "Like he is about to devour a feast?"

He chuckled. "Not a feast—just one, very delicious, set of lips." He bent his head down, and she met him in the middle.

Their kiss sparked a longing in him, and he had to pull away. "If only we were getting married today."

"Our turn will come soon enough." She turned and gazed out the window again.

He nodded. "What were you looking at?"

"I wasn't looking at anything, just thinking about the Banbury Stone."

"Oh?"

"It really is enchanted, is it not? I wished for your love, and it came true."

Anton smiled. "It's nice to think so. But a greater force was at work here. When God wants two people to be together, he doesn't let a little spider get in his way. No web is too great for him to break."

"You believe we were meant to be together? Like Adam and Eve?"

Anton fingered the little curl by her temple. "I believe God answered my prayer when I asked him for you. And I know you make me feel complete."

Her eyes filled with moisture. "And I know love is stronger than fear."

Their lips met again in a mutual promise to always remember what love had taught them.

THE END

Author's Note

I HOPE YOU ENJOYED Elena and Anton's story as much as I enjoyed writing it! These two characters both longed for happiness and finally found it together. Love has a way of healing even the deepest of wounds and filling them up with hope, comfort, and new beginnings. Many of you waited years for Anton's story, and thanks to your emails and messages of encouragement, I am pleased to finally have it your hands. I hope it met with your satisfaction!

The Earl and Miss Muffet, as you likely guessed, is a retelling and reimaging of the nursery rhyme The *Little Miss Muffet*. I have always adored retellings! The history behind nursery rhymes is quite fascinating, and the poem of Miss Muffet is no exception. When Dr. Thomas Muffet penned the rhyme in the sixteenth century (first printed in 1805), I wonder if he knew his words would be memorialized in the minds of children and adults centuries later. Miss Muffet is speculated to be either his daughter Patience (he had two stepdaughters) or Mary, Queen of Scots, who was frightened by a religious reformer.

Since Dr. Muffet was a renowned entomologist, there is also quite the speculation about the spider in the story. It was likely a spider, as the poem says, or a mole cricket—a rather frightening cricket with clawed front legs. There are many wild accounts that Dr. Muffet used spiders in his treatments of the sick, which would have scared away any little girl. Other names for Miss Muffet are Miss Mopsey, Miss Man, and Mary Ester. I personally prefer Miss Elena Muffet, soon to be Lady Crawford.

To those who are being bullied,

Hope can be found.

Text CONNECT to 741741 to reach the Crisis Text Line

ALSO BY ANNEKA R. WALKER

Stand-Alone Novels:

Brides and Brothers

Love in Disguise

Refining the Debutante

Matchmaking Mamas:

Bargaining for the Barrister

An Unwitting Alliance

The Gentleman's Confession

The Rules of Matrimony

Enchanted Regency:

The Masked Baron

The Dreaming Beauty

The Lady Glass

Regency Ever After Novellas:

Her Three Suitors

Lady Mary Contrary

The Earl and Miss Muffet

Christmas Books in Multi-author series:

Merry Kismet

Married By Twelfth Night

Christmas Anthologies:

A Hopeful Christmas

Meet Me Under the Mistletoe

The Holly and the Ivy

A Christmas Serenade

Timeless Romance Anthology:

To Kiss a Wallflower

Anneka R. Walker is a best-selling author of historical and contemporary romance. With humor and an abundance of heart, she crafts uplifting stories you won't soon forget. She is the winner of the Swoony Award, the LDSPMA Praiseworthy Award, and various chapter contests. Her books have received praise from Publishers Weekly, Historical Novel Society, Midwest Book Review, and Readers Favorite. She graduated from Brigham Young University-Idaho with a Bachelor's degree in English and history and hopes to never stop learning. She is a blessed wife, proud mother of five, follower of Jesus, connoisseur of chocolate, and believer in happy endings.

Follow the Author

If you liked this book, please consider leaving a review. They are vital to any book's success.

Stay in touch! I love connecting with my readers!

Subscribe to Anneka's Newsletter:
mailchi.mp/a278fdec4416/authorannekawalker

Facebook: @AnnekaRWalker
Instagram: @authorannekawalker

www.annekawalker.com

Sources

All Bible quotes came from the King James Version of the Bible.

Milton, John. *Paradise Lost*. Public Domain Poetry— *Paradise Lost*— Book I by John Milton. Accessed June 23, 2020. https://www.public-domain-poetry.com/john-milton/paradise-lost-book-i-8312.

Coleridge, Samuel. "The Rime of the Ancient Mariner (in Seven Parts)." Public Domain Poetry— The Rime of the Ancient Mariner (in Seven Parts) by Samuel Taylor Coleridge. Accessed June 23, 2020. https://www.public-domain-poetry.com/samuel-taylor-coleridge/rime-of-the-ancient-mariner-in-seven-parts-7338.

Swift, Jonathan. "GULLIVER'S TRAVELS into Several Remote Nations of the World." Gulliver's Travels, by Jonathan Swift, February 20, 1997. https://www.gutenberg.org/files/829/829-h/829-h.htm.

Shakespeare, William. *The Tempest*, October 26, 2007. https://www.gutenberg.org/files/23042/23042-h/23042-h.htm.

Locke, John. "An Essay Concerning Humane Understanding, Volume I., by John Locke, January 6, 2004. http://www.gutenberg.org/files/10615/10615-h/10615-h.htm.

Printed in Dunstable, United Kingdom